I0823981

UNDISCLOSED

UNDISCLOSED

Aya de León

CANDLEWICK PRESS

First edition 2025

Library of Congress Control Number: pending
ISBN 978-1-5362-3934-8

25 26 27 28 29 30 SHD 10 9 8 7 6 5 4 3 2 1

Printed in Chelsea, MI, USA

This book was typeset in Warnock Pro.

Candlewick Press
99 Dover Street
Somerville, Massachusetts 02144

www.candlewick.com

EU Authorized Representative: HackettFlynn Ltd,
36 Cloch Choirneal, Balrothery, Co. Dublin, K32 C942, Ireland.
EU@walkerpublishinggroup.com

To all the women, particularly those in my family,
whose music moves me and keeps me inspired, and
in memory of Josephine Baker, who smuggled Allied
secrets during World War II in her sheet music

PROLOGUE

Millston, Georgia

I was running out of air.

Usually, I appreciated my body more in the water than on land. The curves in my hips, thighs, and torso were guaranteed to help me float. But floating was exactly what I *didn't* want right now. Because somewhere above me was a guy with a gun, an angry young man who was looking for me. And the only thing hiding me was the cold Georgia river.

I huddled in a tight ball beneath the surface, my heart beating wildly. In scary situations, I usually inhale and exhale slowly to calm myself, but not being able to breathe was precisely my problem. My lungs started to burn with the lack of oxygen, and I felt frantic to take a breath.

I didn't know if the gunman could see me in the water or not. Maybe staying beneath the surface would keep me safe from the bullets, but I didn't have gills. I needed to go up for air or I'd drown.

Unclenching my body, I said a silent prayer and kicked toward the surface, to whatever glinting metal fate might await me there.

The mission wasn't supposed to involve water or guns. It was supposed to be a simple heist, with multiple contingency plans to keep everyone safe. I didn't even have the most dangerous role. It had all started the afternoon before . . .

"I'd like to register to vote," I told the lady with stiff hair and a slightly sour expression.

I slid my passport across the counter, and she peered at it through a pair of glasses on a chain around her neck. It wasn't really my passport; my name is Amani Kendall, and this was Denita Burrell's passport. But it had my photograph and today's date, putting me at exactly eighteen years old.

The stiff-haired lady peered at me over her glasses. I was only fifteen, so I had on glasses of my own and makeup to make me look older. I was tall and plus-size, so no one had thought I was younger than my age since I had made it to double digits.

I saw my reflection in her lenses: oval brown face, large eyes, eager smile—a newly eighteen-year-old Black girl excited to be enfranchised.

And even though the passport wasn't mine, it was

as real as could be. I work for an organization that had had someone at the actual passport office make it and put it in the government files.

Which is why it was so outrageous when she handed the passport back to me. "I'm sorry," she said. "We only accept Georgia identification."

"Excuse me?" I asked. "This is a United States passport."

"It was issued in Los Angeles," she said, "which is a far cry from Millston, Georgia."

"But all my residence documentation is in order," I argued.

"I'm sorry," she said. "Come back when you have a state ID. Next!"

She beckoned to a white woman with two kids behind me, and I stepped to the side.

The glasses lady had done the exact thing we had expected her to do, the thing I was there to catch her doing. And I had. In the upper corners of my glasses' round frames were two smooth blue stones, and the one on the left was a fully functional video camera. The oversize eyewear worked triple duty. The glasses made me look older, they disguised my face a bit, and most important, they were documenting this outrageous voter suppression.

I should have been triumphant, but instead I was furious. How many other Black people had come into this government office and been turned down?

• • •

"It's perfect!" my dad said later that night as he and my mom reviewed the footage from the glasses cam.

My father, mother, and I sat at the kitchen table in a house the Factory had rented for us—a cozy bungalow on a tree-lined street, only a short walk from the county office.

I sat beside my dad. He was taller than me, with a long and lean figure. For this assignment, he was clean-shaven, with his hair cut in a low fade. The haircut was supposed to make him look serious, but right now, his face was all excitement.

"Look at this," he said, pointing to the video. "You really linger on your brown hands setting the passport on the desk, but your thumb is covering the perfect amount of your face in the photo." He grinned across the table at Mom. "We'll totally be able to use this."

Mom was brushing out her wig on a Styrofoam wig head. It looked like I was facing two women: above was Mom, with her hair cornrowed back; below was the second head, a ghost-white face that implied features, the wig straight and brown, with just a bump of curl where it grazed the table.

"Agreed," my mother said. "Are you all ready for part two?"

Dad and I nodded. Our family worked as a team for the Factory, an international espionage agency dedicated to fighting racism, and this was our first mission in the South. We were investigating reports of voter suppression in Georgia. Not only were people of color being turned away from registering to vote, but we suspected that this same county office was also destroying many of the voter registration forms that they accepted.

Mom turned the wig around to inspect it. She nodded and set down the brush. "Get some rest," Mom said. "We have a big day tomorrow."

At nine a.m. sharp, I was back at the county office. The same woman stood at the desk. When she saw me, her expression went from slightly sour to full-on lemon.

"I certainly hope you're not here with that same out-of-state identification," she said.

"I looked on the internet," I said. "And according to Georgia's secretary of state, I have the right to use this identification to vote."

"Missy," she said, "stop wasting everybody's time."

"Wasting whose time?" I asked. "There's no one else here."

As if to prove me wrong, a woman walked in, but she wasn't a customer. She had on a custodian uniform, with a cap low over her eyes. I recognized Mom from the telltale straight, shoulder-length brown hair. Dad—the third member of our team—was out front in the van.

"The only person getting their time wasted is me,"

I said to the woman at the desk. "Since you're not doing your job."

Now her expression went from sour to furious. "I have half a mind to call the police on you."

Her eyes were locked on to mine as my mom pushed past the low wooden swinging door and walked behind the counter. She emptied a few wastebaskets into a translucent plastic bag.

I continued to argue with the woman at the desk as my mother made her way to the back of the office. In the rear was a large shredder. Mom set down the translucent bag and proceeded to empty the contents of the shredder into a black garbage bag.

As I argued, my glasses cam caught everything on video that my mom did.

My mom walked back out through the wooden swinging half door, and the woman behind the counter and I both turned to her. "Louise," she said, "would you please call security?"

Mom nodded and pulled out her phone. "We need you to come on in," she said. "There's a problem."

I kept the phone cam pointed at the bag.

"We'll see how much you like getting sent to the county jail for voter fraud," the woman said to me.

"Did someone say voter fraud?" a tall white guy in a suit asked, walking in the front door.

"Yes," my mom said, opening the plastic bag. "These

destroyed materials were confiscated from the shredder in this county office."

I kept the glasses cam on Mom's hands and the bag, but not on her face.

"You're not Louise," the desk woman said, outraged.

"No, ma'am," she said.

"You can't just come in here and remove government property," the woman said. "That's illegal search and seizure."

"As a point of fact," the man in the suit said, "the *police* aren't allowed to conduct illegal searches and seizures. But a private citizen is telling me that these shredded documents were confiscated from this office, and as a county commissioner, it is my sworn duty to look into those allegations."

"I don't know what's in that bag," the woman sputtered. "I've never seen those papers before in my life. She could have brought those in from anywhere."

"Actually," I said, "we got it all on camera. From the moment my associate took them from the county shredder to the moment that this county commissioner took possession of them. It's called a chain of custody."

"I'll tell you who's going to end up in custody," the woman said, pointing at Mom. "This thief right here."

A security guard appeared then, and the woman turned to him. "Arrest this woman!" she demanded.

"Ms. Harlowe," the county commissioner said to

the desk woman, "you're just making things worse."

The security guard looked from the tall man in the suit to Ms. Harlowe.

"Ms. Harlowe, I—" he began.

"Who got you this job, Parnell?" she demanded. "Who pays your salary?"

"I'm sorry," the guard said. I'm not sure if he was speaking to the man in the suit or to my mom.

This wasn't supposed to happen. The county commissioner was supposed to take over, and we were supposed to walk out, victorious.

"Hold on," I said. "You're arresting this woman?" I raised my voice. "For taking out the garbage? On garbage day?"

Our team had selected garbage day so the staff would be expecting someone to pick up the trash. But I was speaking extra loud so that Dad—who could hear me through the communicators—would understand what was happening.

"Is it a crime in Georgia to take out recycling?" I demanded of Ms. Harlowe. "Or just to try to register to vote if you're Black?"

"I've had just about enough of you," Ms. Harlowe said.

Parnell, the security guard, had my mom in cuffs. Where was Dad?

"If you arrest this woman, you'll need to arrest me, too," I said loudly.

Parnell looked to Ms. Harlowe. "I only got one set of cuffs."

"Just take the thief," she said. "Lock her in the office until the police get here."

"I need an assist in the front lobby," Parnell said into his radio.

The county commissioner had his camera phone out and was documenting the whole thing. "This is outrageous," he said. "There will definitely be repercussions."

A second security guard came into the lobby. He had a pair of cuffs out and was advancing toward me.

I backed away from him as the front door opened, and a tall, clean-shaven Black man wearing a suit—Dad!—strode in with a camerawoman. He spoke into a handheld microphone: "We're here on the scene in the county government office, where we've received reports of voter suppression. And it appears that someone is in custody? Commissioner, we're live. What's going on?"

I was so relieved Dad had arrived. He would make sure Mom didn't get arrested.

The camerawoman swept her lens across the lobby as the county commissioner talked about all that had happened. The security guard froze in his tracks, and I slipped out the door.

"Head back to the house, Amani," Mom whispered into the communicators. "Dad can take it from here. We'll meet you at HQ."

I walked down the county office steps and hurried

up the street. In my ear, Ms. Harlowe sputtered about Georgia's glorious legacy being ruined. Statues being taken down. Outsiders coming in, trying to tell people what to do. Liberals reporting fake news.

A recycling truck passed by, and for a minute I couldn't hear.

Then I heard Dad asking loudly in his reporter voice, "But what is this woman being charged with?"

"Like that young lady said," the county commissioner's voice came through my earpiece, "if this woman gets arrested, they'll have to take me, too. Because I— Hey! Wait!"

I was at the end of the block, but I swiveled back toward the county office. What was going on? Did they need my help?

A teenage boy, maybe slightly older than me, came running out the door with the black garbage bag. Dad came running out after him.

The recycling truck was idling at the curb. The kid swung the garbage bag into the back of the truck and jumped on board. He put the truck in gear and sped off.

The man who worked for waste management looked up, startled, from the bin he was wheeling into the street.

Dad was too far behind, and the truck was about to pass me. As it came closer, I didn't think. I just knew I couldn't let our evidence disappear. I took three running steps and leaped up onto the back of the truck.

We weren't going superfast, but it was too fast for Dad to catch up. And the kid was driving away from downtown. Where was he going?

"Amani," Dad said, his voice urgent through the communicator, "are you okay?"

"I'm on the truck!" I whispered. "We're going down a wide street, but it's all industrial."

"I'm tracking your signal," he said. "The kid is probably headed for the interstate. We can't let him get on the freeway."

"What can I do?" I asked. "There are no lights or stop signs on this street. There's no one around. Should I just grab the bag and bail out?"

I saw the concrete speeding past. I was afraid I'd break a leg if I tried to jump off the truck. Plus, the kid might stop the truck and come after me. I'd never be able to outrun him with a sprained ankle. Even if I didn't injure myself, it would be hard to run with a huge bag of shredded paper.

"I have an idea," Dad said. "There's a bridge coming up. It goes over a river. You should be able to jump."

"Jump?"

"It isn't high up," he said. "It's your best bet."

"I guess it's better than concrete," I said.

"Move to the extreme right of the truck," he said. "Take the bag."

I grabbed it. My palms were sweating so much that

the plastic was slippery in my hands. Unfortunately, the bag didn't have a drawstring—it was just a rectangle of black plastic.

"Can you see the bridge?" Dad asked.

"I'm afraid to stick my head out," I said. "The guy might be able to see me in his mirror."

"Good point," Dad said. "The bridge is coming up in another block or so."

I tightened my hands on the slippery plastic. It occurred to me that not only would I get wet but the papers would, too. And the glasses cam. That couldn't happen!

I tossed the glasses in with the shredded paper, then hooked my arm around the truck's handle. Now that my other hand was free, I twisted the top of the bag and tied it into a knot, pulling as tight as my sweaty grip would allow.

And then, suddenly, the road turned into a bridge.

Dad was right—the river was not far below—but what he hadn't factored in were the steel girders holding up the bridge blocking my way. They had gaps between them, but the driver had picked up speed.

I missed the first opening, and then there were more girders blocking me from the water. It was like double Dutch—I had to figure out when to jump. I was only going to get three chances. The first one had whipped by. I peeked out around the side of the truck and felt the wind in my face. My heart pounded in my throat as the second opening flashed past. If I didn't jump on this third one, it was going to be concrete for me.

I leaned forward and gripped the bag. This was it! Pushing off with my legs, I leaped clear. But the bag bumped against the girder, and it whipped toward me, knocking me backward. My body was in a sitting position when I hit the water, making a huge splash.

As the cold river swallowed me, I gripped the bag with both hands. My head went under, but the bag acted like a flotation device, pulling me back up. My sodden clothes and shoes turned heavy, weighing me down. The communicator slipped out of my ear and fell, sinking toward the bottom of the river.

Surfacing, I shook my head and blinked the water from my eyes. As my vision cleared, I saw that the guy had stopped the truck and was running toward the edge of the bridge. *Ha!* I thought as I floated away with the bag. But then he reached into his waistband and pulled out a gun.

What? No! I took in a lungful of air and ducked my head under the water. Holding my breath, I hid below the bag. What did I think that would do? Stop a bullet?

My heart hammered in my chest. I had taken a deep breath, but I was running out of oxygen. I imagined the bullet zinging into the water. Even if it missed me, it would hit the bag and deflate it, allowing the water to seep in and ruin all our evidence.

I stayed under for as long as I could, until my lungs

burned, and I felt frantic to breathe. I came up for air, expecting to hear a shot. But it was quiet. The guy was gone. Another car had come up behind the truck, and the county commissioner was stepping out of the driver's side. Mom and Dad were stepping out of the back. I waved to them from the water. Even from a distance, I could see the lines in my parents' posture go from tense to relaxed.

I tied the bag of papers to me with the drawstring of my sweatpants, and then I swam to shore.

ONE

Two days after my parents pulled me out of a Georgia river, I woke up at "home." I put "home" in air quotes these days, because my family has been living in a series of furnished apartments and houses throughout the US. We haven't had a permanent residence since our house in LA burned down, which is a whole other story.

Dad knocked on my bedroom door. "You up, honey?"

"Yeah," I murmured. "Getting up." I looked around, slightly disoriented. Everything in the apartment was in shades of white and beige. At our real home, things had been much more colorful.

"Jerrold has something for us," Dad said. "Can you be downstairs in fifteen?"

The clock read 8:45. "Yep," I said, rubbing my eyes.

Jerrold is our handler at the International Alternative Intelligence Consortium (IAIC), better known as the Factory. I'd learned less than a year ago that my parents had secretly been spies my whole life. Some people might say that makes my whole childhood a lie . . . welp, the jury is still out on that one.

But it's hard to be too angry when I think about the important work the Factory does—fighting racism and protecting people of color around the world. Now that I'm part of the operation, I've gone through short-term, extensive spy training, and my family has gone on several missions together. Our latest apartment is in Florida, because Mom speaks fluent Spanish and often our work takes us to Latin America and the Caribbean.

But that morning, I knew the next mission wouldn't be for Mom. She was still in Georgia, being deposed by the attorneys for the legal case about the voter suppression. There were butterflies in my stomach as I wondered what might be in store for me.

At nine a.m., I was sitting at the kitchen table and looking at Jerrold on a videoconference screen. He seemed the same as always, crisp and professional in a suit, his brown eyes looking through silver-framed glasses on his earnest brown face.

"Your mother should be back soon," Jerrold said. "Her testimony will make this an open-and-shut case when it goes to trial. They may call Amani to the stand about the shooting, but that won't be for months, at least. What matters now is that you all did really great work in Georgia."

"Thanks," Dad said. He had a five o'clock shadow on his chin. Now that he was no longer playing a newscaster, he didn't have to be quite so clean-shaven. "What's next for us?"

"Not so much you, Forrest," Jerrold said. "This next mission is really for Amani."

"Me?" I asked. I'd wondered if that was a possibility. The summer had been back-to-back missions so far, and I hadn't been expecting something new so soon, let alone my first time being the primary operative as an officially trained Factory spy. I sat up straighter in my chair.

"Absolutely," Jerrold said. "We think you'd be ideal for this assignment. It seems that . . . Actually, let me just share my screen."

He pulled up a photo of a Black mother and daughter. "This is Danielle Hunter and her mother, Sheila."

The girl was around my age. Her mom looked to be in her late thirties or early forties. Same long slender frames, same large brown eyes. "Sheila and her late husband, Thomas, were Factory operatives," Jerrold continued. "Danielle is sixteen years old. She's the assignment. Sheila no longer works for us. She has a job at Execu-Fetch."

"Is that another intelligence agency?" I asked.

"No, honey," Dad said. "It's a next-level rideshare for wealthy businesspeople. Limos, private jets, that sort of thing."

Jerrold pulled up a video. "This is an interview with Sheila from a few months ago."

In the video, the mom, Sheila, came in and sat down at a table. She was neatly dressed in a sweater and slacks. Jerrold sat across from her.

"Sheila," Jerrold said, "thanks for contacting us. We never did get a chance to do your exit interview. But I understand, given the circumstances with Thomas. And I'm surprised that you've come in now, considering the hurricane."

"She found it!" Sheila burst out, burying her head in her hands.

"Who found what?" Jerrold asked.

"My daughter, Danielle." Sheila was sobbing now, her words hard to understand. "In the wall. I had hidden it, but I never expected . . ."

In the video, Jerrold reached over to a side table and handed Sheila a tissue. The live Jerrold hit fast-forward. "I'm skipping the part where her words were inaudible," he said, then hit play again.

"Please, Sheila," Jerrold was saying in the video, "start from the beginning. What happened?"

"After Thomas died, I just had to get away," she said. "I moved Danielle and myself to Hawaii. I bought a house with the life insurance. And before we moved in, I did a little bit of 'remodeling.'" She put the last word in air quotes. "I took the box of sensitive documents about Thomas, and I—I plastered it into a wall. I couldn't bear to look at it, but I also couldn't bear to destroy it. It had all the documents from our life with the Factory. I couldn't leave it around for Danielle to find. I even had instructions in my will about what to do with the box in case I died. Because it had Thomas's death certificate. It said that he died from a gunshot wound." Her tears began again.

"You hadn't told Danielle?" he asked.

"I said he died in a car accident," she explained. "I couldn't tell her at the time—I just couldn't. She was too young. Too heartbroken about his death. I kept telling myself I would tell her later. I thought maybe when she was eighteen. But I waited too long. Because then the hurricane came and left the house half-destroyed." She reached for another tissue.

"Go on," Jerrold prompted gently.

"A tree fell on the house and crushed the whole wall," Sheila said. "The box was in a pile of rubble and Danielle found it. But it wasn't just the papers she found. As a kid, she had been on assignment with us. There were photos of Thomas and his partner—" There was a glitch in the video there. Clearly, Jerrold had redacted the partner's name. "She was a smart girl. She remembered him—he was a close friend of our family, close enough that she used to call him 'uncle.' She asked me directly—she was pleading for the truth—*How did my father die? He was shot?* I couldn't lie to her anymore. I explained that we were spies, including"—glitch—"and that her father died in the line of duty."

In the video, Jerrold's eyes were filled with compassion. I had never seen that look on his face before; he was always crisp and professional. But I had never lost anyone in the line of duty. Hopefully, I never would.

"Again," Jerrold said, "I'm so sorry for your loss. Thomas was a good man and a good spy. I'm sure Danielle was inconsolable when he first passed. This has to have been quite a shock. Where did you leave things with her?"

"I gave her a chance to settle down," Sheila said. "And I explained how important the Factory's work is. I emphasized how much she needs to protect our organization."

"Do you think she understands?" Jerrold asked.

"I think she does," Sheila said.

Jerrold stopped the video.

"And that was where we left it," he said. "Until we saw this . . ."

He pulled up another screen. It was an Instagram video. Several girls were in a living room at a party. The lights were dim. But not so dim that I couldn't see the mess of red plastic cups on the coffee table.

There were five teen girls in the video. One was Danielle, sitting with two dark-haired girls of indeterminate race, a blond girl, and an East Asian girl.

Jerrold unmuted, and loud music played in the background. One of the dark-haired girls was talking, but she was farthest away from the camera phone, so I didn't quite understand what she said. Suddenly, all of them laughed.

"The audio isn't great," Jerrold said. "But we enhanced it for the relevant portions."

Then Danielle began talking. She wore glittery eye shadow and had her hair in a short, straight bob.

"My two truths and a lie?" Danielle asked, then threw back her head and laughed. From the wildness of her laugh and her wobbly posture, I gathered she was pretty drunk.

"One? I'm terrified of singing in public," she said, ticking them off on her fingers. "Two? I've never had a pet of any kind. And three? My mother is a spy for a rogue organization."

"Three!" most of the girls said.

"No!" the Asian girl said. "It's one! I've seen Danielle sing in public. She has an amazing voice."

"But then her parents would have to be spies," the blond girl said. "Which is ridiculous."

"Yeah," the other dark-haired girl said. "You can still sing in public even if you're terrified."

"Three!" the blond girl began chanting. "Three! Three!"

Most of the girls joined in: "THREE! THREE!"

Danielle began to laugh so hard, it verged on hysteria. "Okay," she said, her eyes streaming with tears of laughter. "It was just too ridiculous. Whose parents are spies, right? That's the one. Three is the lie."

The video ended. I think my mouth was still open in shock.

"Technically, it is a lie," Jerrold said. "Her parents *were* spies with us."

"But how could she just say that?" I asked. "And on social media?"

In my recent training, it had been stressed to us over and over again that the only way the Factory can continue its work is to stay under the radar.

"Sheila thinks Danielle blames the Factory for her father's death," Jerrold said.

"Was it the Factory's fault?" I asked.

Jerrold let out a breath. "Spycraft is dangerous work, and sometimes we do lose agents," he said. "If her father had been an accountant, he would probably be alive today. But we carefully investigated the operation, as we do anytime an agent is seriously injured or killed. We did an extensive debriefing with his partner. We took every precaution, followed every safety protocol, and there was no negligence in the operation. But the hurricane was traumatic. And the grief of losing their house, plus learning the real circumstances of her dad's death, has ripped open the grief of losing him all over again. Sometimes grieving people are looking for someone to blame."

"So maybe she's sorry/not sorry for letting something slip," I said.

"Yes," Jerrold said. "And it gets worse." He moved the mouse arrow on his screen until it hovered over one of the dark-haired girls. "This young woman is the daughter of a local police chief. If Danielle discloses too much, there's a direct line to law enforcement."

I knew how dangerous that was. If the wrong people in the FBI or CIA were to learn about us, we would likely be labeled an extremist organization, even though the Factory uses only nonviolent strategies, focusing mainly on gathering information, leaking it to the press, and helping whistleblowers.

"I can understand why you're concerned about these security breaches," Dad said.

"Sheila has caught Danielle sneaking out at night and suspects she's been drinking. We asked Sheila to talk to Danielle and to reiterate our concerns. This is an audio recording that Sheila made of that conversation."

"Hey, sweetheart," came Sheila's voice, "can we check in before you go?"

"Check in about what?" Danielle's voice was sullen.

"About . . . security," Sheila said. "The Factory—"

"Oh my God, Mom," Danielle said. "No one cares about your stupid Factory, okay?"

"Okay, but can you just promise me that you won't say anything about it to anyone?"

"Again?" Danielle said. "Believe me, no one cares."

"I'm not sure about that," Sheila said. "Honey, I know it's been a lot of change lately—"

"Change?" Danielle said, sounding more and more upset. "Basically, my life has crashed and burned . . . twice. First Dad died. Then, just as I was getting over that, there's this hurricane. Now I'm stuck in this tiny apartment with you breathing down my neck every single second." There was a sound like her hand had slammed down on the table. "I hate it here!"

I could hear the desperation in Danielle's voice. She was mad, but she also sounded like she might be on the verge of tears.

"Sweetheart," Sheila said, "it's been a lot. It would be too much for anyone. I think . . . I mean, I hope you'll look into getting some support. Would you please consider talking to a counselor?"

"Oh, *I'm* the one who needs counseling?" Danielle said. "You can forget about that plan. I'm not gonna go pour my heart out to some therapist while you just go and throw yourself into your new Execu-Fetch promotion and act like nothing happened. Exactly like you did when Dad died!"

"Danielle!" Sheila said. "That's not fair!"

"I hate you!" Danielle screamed. "I hate this place!"

I heard running footsteps and Sheila calling

"Danielle! Danielle!" The voice got farther away until a door slammed and the recording stopped.

Across the table, my own dad's brow was furrowed, and his jaw was tight. "That's not good at all."

"And there's more," Jerrold said. "Right now, her father's former partner is in an active operation that is getting a lot of heat."

Dad nodded, his frown deepening. "So not only is Danielle in a position to blow the Factory's cover generally by letting people know it exists, but she's also a direct link to her father's former partner at a particularly delicate moment."

"Exactly," Jerrold said. "And Danielle is right about her mother. Sheila was a good spy because she could keep her feelings contained and controlled. So when she was suddenly widowed, she didn't take time to process everything—instead, she abruptly left us and swept Danielle off to a new life. Now that life is falling apart, and we worry that Danielle is falling apart along with it."

"This is a serious internal threat," Dad said.

"The night of this last audio recording," Jerrold said, "Danielle didn't come home. We upped the security, and a Factory operative had Danielle under surveillance the following day. But she managed to elude him."

"Does Danielle have spy training?" I asked.

"A limited amount. Her parents had her in

self-defense courses when they were active," Jerrold said. "And unfortunately, it seems to be kicking in. Our new strategy is to have someone handle her."

Dad and I looked at each other.

"Me," I said.

"Bingo," Jerrold said. "We don't think Danielle will actually say anything about the Factory publicly. If we did, we'd extract her immediately. But we can't take a chance. We need you to assess the situation and let us know whether she's a threat or not. Ideally, you'd talk to her and convince her to seek counseling. But mostly, you just need to let us know what you learn."

Sounded simple enough. "So I'm going to Hawaii?"

Jerrold smiled. "Not quite that far west," he said. "If you agree to take on this mission, you'll start the day after tomorrow. Danielle is in a band. They're going to audition for a summer competition camp. Most of the auditions are taking place in Los Angeles, but there are some bands—like Danielle's—that need a lead singer."

"I would have to sing?" I asked.

Jerrold nodded. "If you agree to the mission, we'll enter you in the contest as a vocalist."

My eyes widened. "Okay," I said weakly. I liked to sing, and my parents always told me I had a good voice, but I'd never sung in front of a crowd before.

"We want you to make contact at the audition in San Diego," he said. "Give us an initial progress report. If possible, join her band and help them pass the audition.

The music camp would be an ideal contained environment, where you could keep a close eye on Danielle over a period of time."

"So I'm just watching and reporting?" I asked.

"We want you to assess the threat level," Jerrold said. "Best-case scenario: Danielle seems stable and the threat has passed."

"I'm hoping for that one," Dad said.

"Second-best-case scenario," Jerrold said. "Danielle isn't stable, but you might be able to convince her to seek support around her grief. Our hope is that if she can address the underlying issues, she won't be as volatile."

"Therapy was a hard pass in the conversation with Sheila," Dad said.

"Teenagers are often more easily swayed by peers than parents," Jerrold said. "We have a Factory therapist who specializes in helping people through grief."

"A spy?" I asked.

"No," Jerrold said. "She's a real therapist. Everything would be confidential unless Danielle posed a threat to herself or others."

Phew. I didn't like the idea of sending a teenager to a fake therapist who would be reporting their sessions.

"Those are the best outcomes," Jerrold said. "But if neither of these scenarios work, then we'll have to extract her."

"Extract her to where?" I asked.

"We would relocate Danielle outside the US and put her completely off the grid."

"Whoa," I said, imagining being suddenly yanked out of my life and sent to another country with no way of keeping in touch with any of my friends back home. This had happened to some friends of mine earlier in the year. I was determined not to let it happen again.

"It wouldn't be permanent," Jerrold said. "But at least as long as her father's former partner is involved in his current mission. Extracting and deporting Danielle and her mother would be a last resort, but we can't take the risk of her exposing our organization. We hope it won't come to that."

I had no question about accepting the mission. I believed in the Factory and would fight to protect it. And I felt for this girl whose life had been blown up twice. I hoped to keep it from being blown up a third time.

But music camp? A vocal audition? Apparently, my parents had pulled me out of muddy Georgia water only to head to a drought-ravaged California, where the mission would depend on my ability to sing.

Two

According to her file, Danielle Colette Hunter was sixteen and going to be a junior. In the file photo, she stared sullenly at the camera with dark brown eyes in a face the color of warm chestnut. Her long extension braids were pulled back into a ponytail, and she wore a sports jersey from her school's junior varsity soccer team.

En route from Florida to San Diego, when I wasn't sleeping, I was studying Danielle's photo. And from the moment the plane touched down, I was looking for her. In the airport. In the rideshare. And certainly when I arrived at the music school where the tryouts were being held.

There was a table just outside the door where I signed in.

"Name, please?" the cheerful redhead at the table asked.

So my real name is Amani Kendall, but I gave them the name I use when I'm undercover.

"Imani Kennedy," I said.

It's perfect because the first name is close enough that I always know to answer when someone calls my name. But the different spellings of the first name and different last name means no one will ever find me in a search.

"Vocalist or group member?" the redhead asked.

"Vocalist," I said.

She handed me a small flyer with a QR code. "Here is your selection survey. It has the band audition videos and their rankings. You'll pick your top three for initial interviews. A sort of band speed dating. If you like them and they like you, it's a match. If you don't get matched up with anyone, you may need to pick a band that's not your first choice, or else try again next time. But assuming you do get matched up, you and your new band will have the rest of today and most of tomorrow to prepare for your audition."

I thanked her and followed the signs in through the auditorium doors.

It was a standard high school cafeteria: high ceilings with acoustic tile, linoleum floors, and folding tables with benches. And it was packed full of teens repping all genres of music.

I wandered toward the food table. I got a can of juice and a sandwich, then continued scanning the crowd for Danielle. I saw lots of different hair colors and plenty of denim, leather, and sparkles, but no Danielle.

Finally, I spotted her at a table in the front near the stage, but there weren't any open spots near her. Maybe if I was super skinny, I could have squeezed in at a nearby table, but my hips required some real space.

I found a seat, and on either side of me were other vocalists looking at the QR code website, studying the bands. I didn't have to study much, since I already knew who I wanted to match with. Danielle's band was called "The Quad." I selected them and tried to submit my form, but I got an error message saying I had to select two others. I clicked on the first two that said R & B or hip-hop, then hit submit.

Soon after I had finished, a middle-aged woman with half-glasses stepped up to the podium onstage. "Welcome, everyone, to the band and vocalist matchups for *The Next Teen Sensation*," she said, and everyone clapped.

She repeated much of what I had learned in my briefing—that this was a talent scouting venture like *American Idol* or *The Voice*, where bands would get a shot at the big time. There were at least seventy-five teens in the room, and all of them (except me) had come from the West Coast or Hawaii. There were another two hundred teens at the audition in Los Angeles. From these Southern California auditions, only ten bands would be chosen for the next round, to go to camp in Portland, Oregon. At camp, they would each get intensive support and mentoring to come up with an original song, and then there would be another competition where the top band would be chosen. The winning band would go on to the final round in Northern California against bands from all over the US. The winner would be crowned by the K-pop band sensation Sound Cake. A record contract wasn't a guarantee, but the audience at the finals would be full of scouts for all the record labels. In other words, it was a really big deal.

"Bands are all about chemistry," the woman at the podium was explaining. "BTS, the Spice Girls, One Direction . . . producers have been combining total strangers into groups and turning them into massive hitmakers for years. All of you are here because, based on your audition videos, we thought your band had potential and, with the right singer, you had a shot at winning. Some of you will compete as is, but many of you are here to find a new lead singer. So, yes, you may have had to say goodbye to some of your friends . . . but your friends may not have what it takes. This process prepares you for the real world—the competition is stiff. Don't let anyone hold you back. It's a small price to pay to make it to the next level."

Yikes. What happened to "Music is fun"? "Have a good time"? This was a hypercompetitive environment. It was the last place I would want an emotionally volatile young woman without a handler.

We were all dismissed to go to our assigned rehearsal spaces. The app told me I was supposed to start with a hip-hop band called "Illumiknotty," which was on the east end of the music building. But instead, I walked out the cafeteria's south exit, following Danielle. She was with two other girls, and they were looking at their phones, walking across the school grounds between several blocky buildings.

They entered what looked like a science center. I assumed they were heading to their assigned room. Following them, I continued to the other end of the hallway and out the exit door, then walked around the side of the building and peeked in the window.

They were in a large classroom, with sinks and science equipment around the perimeter. Her friends were both girls of color with curly dark hair. One had on a shirt that said NATIVE HAWAIIAN PRIDE. The other girl looked South Asian.

I heard a woman's voice behind me, and I turned, stepping away from the window.

"Excuse me," the redheaded woman called to me. "Are you Haley?"

"Am I—?" I smiled at her. "Uh, no. I was just looking to see if I was in the right place."

She pulled up the app and directed me toward my first speed-dating audition. As I walked away, I heard a perky voice through the window.

"Hi, I'm Haley!"

Inwardly, I hoped that Haley was not a great singer and hurried across the campus.

When I opened the door of my assigned room, I was shocked to see that Illumiknotty, the hip-hop group, was all white. I guess maybe I should have taken more time to look at the bands on the website.

A blond guy with a Tupac T-shirt and a backward baseball cap greeted me. "Peace, my Nubian queen."

"Excuse me?" I asked.

Behind him were two white guys in hoodies and jeans and a blond girl who waved at me. Her platinum hair was braided back in cornrows and she wore bamboo earrings. As she grinned my way, I could see that she had gold grills on both the top and bottom, with a diamond glinting in each tooth.

"Go ahead and sing whatever you prepared," she said. "Do you have a track to play or do you just want to sing a cappella?"

I wanted to get out of there as soon as possible.

"A cappella is fine," I said.

I didn't even wait for the guy in the Tupac shirt to join the rest of them. I just took a deep breath and belted out a Beyoncé song. It wasn't half-bad, but I definitely did not give it my all.

When I was done, the guy in the Tupac shirt looked me dead in the eye. "That was great," he said. "I'm hoping you'll join us and bring some much-needed melanin to our hip-hop aficionado crew."

"Oh, I thought this band did R & B," I said, picking up my backpack. "I guess it's not a match. Sorry. I'm not really into hip-hop." That was a lie. There are lots of types of hip-hop and plenty of them I like. But I wasn't going to tell him that.

"But hip-hop is the sound of Black self-expression," he said. "It's the declaration of a new generation. We can help you find your way back to your roots."

Ugh. "Not interested," I said. "Excuse me."

"There is no excuse for not knowing your culture," he said. "If you can freestyle sixteen bars, I'll let you go."

"You want a freestyle?" I asked. *"This is wack, now please step back."*

"Predictable," he said.

What the—? I was not going to let this— Then, I just closed my eyes and let my mind rip:

> *"Who are you to be so damn commanding?*
> *Claiming hip-hop when you clearly have no*
> *understanding.*

Appropriating culture when it's not your own.
Acting like you'll school me in Blackness and bring
me home.
This ain't your house. Not your lyrics to spit.
This ain't your culture, and you can't have it.
Find your own heritage that you can flex.
That could be your path to real success.
Because right now you're a true hot mess.
You and your white savior hip-hop complex."

I expected him to have an attitude, but he looked at me with deep admiration. "I knew you had the magic." He grinned. "We are not worthy. I hope you'll say yes to us, because we'll definitely be saying yes to you, queen."

I couldn't even say anything. I just walked past him and hurried to my next audition, but though I was using the GPS on the app, I got turned around. Maybe I was sort of shook from that first audition. The nerve of that guy. I guess he got under my skin.

I took a breath. *Just keep moving,* I reminded myself. *Get through these first two auditions. Get to Danielle's band.*

The second audition was in the music building. It was a slightly sullen group of suburban-looking boys, all with dyed hair, who they said they were looking for a female singer. I did the same Beyoncé song. They asked if I had something a bit more alternative, and I said I didn't. Clearly this was not a match. I excused myself and strode back across the campus to the science building until I reached the door with a paper taped to it that said THE QUAD. Danielle's group.

I took a deep breath, then turned the doorknob and walked into the science center classroom, back straight, head up.

"Hi," I said. "My name is Imani, and your band is definitely my first choice."

"Cool," the Hawaiian girl said. "We need a singer, and we haven't had much luck so far. You wanna just jump in?"

I considered my options. I had brought a track to sing along with, and I might sound better with the background music.

My heart was pounding thinking about how much was riding on this. If they didn't choose me, I wouldn't be able to keep an eye on Danielle or do a good job at the assessment.

I looked at their amplifier hookup. There was a speaker and a laptop plugged in. How would I pair my phone with it? Dang, I should have already gotten on the Wi-Fi. Would the delay make the moment even more awkward? It was probably better to go before I could get any more nervous. When my throat is tight, my voice never sounds as good.

I nodded, then took several deep breaths to calm my hammering heart. Finally, I took a big lungful of air and busted out Anasuya Blackwell's anthem:

"This is for all the girls who hesitate
For all the girls with self-hate
You're magic—there's no one else like you
It's tragic—all that you've been through
But you're not alone—your sisters are here to bring you home . . ."

I had to fight to keep my eyes open. I wished I could close them and just be alone with the music. But instead, I focused on the distance, beyond their three faces, and let them be blurry, expressionless.

When I finally finished the song, I took another breath and let my eyes focus on them. I saw three brown girls—eyes wide in admiration.

I could feel my face flush as they were staring at me, all talking at once.

"Wow," Danielle said. "You really can sing."

"Please, please, please, pick us as your first choice," the South Asian girl said.

"You *have* to join our band," the Hawaiian girl said. She introduced herself as Noelani, with she/her pronouns. The South Asian girl was Sarita, also she/her. And of course, I already knew Danielle's name, but she confirmed that her pronouns were she/her.

"Danielle is a great singer, but she gets major stage fright," Noelani said. "So our bass player, Casey, has been singing, and that hasn't been ideal. With you, we've got a shot."

"Seriously," Danielle said. "My anxiety is already through the roof. Singing in public would finish me. I'd be vomiting like the girl in that *Lady Parts* TV show."

"The one about the Muslim punk band?" Sarita asked.

Danielle nodded.

I kind of understood how Danielle felt. I loved to sing in the shower or in the car with the radio on. A couple of times, I had done karaoke with my family to celebrate finishing a mission. But that was always in towns where no one knew me, in front of people I would never see again—other than my parents.

"Hopefully you'll join us," Danielle said. "And I can focus on the keyboard."

"But if not," Noelani said, "*you'll* have to sing for the audition, Danielle."

"Help us, Obi-Wan," Danielle said, like Princess Leia in the original *Star Wars*. "You're our only hope."

THREE

It's funny how different the cafeteria looked when I had someone to eat with. I was a spy, but I still couldn't 100 percent detach myself from social anxiety in groups of teenagers. So even though I was eating with them under false pretenses, I felt better knowing that I had a crew.

When we'd arrived at the cafeteria, the organizers had handed us more packaged sandwiches and announced the new pairings, based on which bands and singers had chosen one another. A bunch of vocalists who hadn't been matched with a band got up and left—this really was a tough business—and the rest of us got down to work. Staff passed around audition sheets for tomorrow's competition, and we filled out the forms over dinner.

I was still on East Coast time, so I was famished, digging into my turkey sandwich with much more fervor than it deserved.

Noelani and Sarita opened their sandwiches and automatically swapped, Noelani ending up with PB&J and Sarita ending up with double turkey.

"So our band needs a new name," Sarita said.

Noelani nodded. "The Quad only worked when there were four of us."

"What about 'The Quint'?" Sarita asked. "Or 'The Quintet'?"

"I like that," said Noelani.

Danielle shook her head. "I originally liked 'The Fly Four,'" she said. "It could just as easily be 'The Fly Five.'"

"We don't like it," Sarita said. "It makes us think of bugs."

"Sarita didn't like it," Danielle said. "And the girlfriends always vote together." She cut her eyes at the two other girls.

I hadn't realized Sarita and Noelani were a couple.

"I like 'The Fly Five,'" Danielle said. "And Casey agrees with me."

I hadn't met Casey, the bass player, yet. Apparently, she was late getting to the audition.

"So we're split down the middle," Noelani said. "'The Fly Five' versus 'The Quintet.' You'll be the tie-breaking vote, Imani."

I finished chewing. "I like them both," I said,

attempting to be diplomatic. "But what about 'The Fierce Five'?"

All three of them shook their heads.

"Too femme," Noelani said. "It sounds too much like girl power."

"What's wrong with girl power?" I asked.

"Casey will never go for that," Danielle said.

"Why not?" I asked, feeling irritated. I hate it when girls don't like to stand up for other girls, or for feminism in general.

But just then, a Black boy walked up and asked, "Casey will never go for what?" Just like a teen boy to barge into a girls' conversation. What was he even doing at our table? I gave him a once-over. He had a sort of cool rock-and-roll vibe, black clothes, and a hairstyle like Erik Killmonger in *Black Panther*.

"Because," Noelani answered me, gesturing at the boy, "he's a guy."

"You're Casey?" I asked, looking at him more closely.

He met my eyes for the first time, and his mouth fell open. "And you're incredibly beautiful," he said.

I swallowed. Was this a joke?

Noelani rolled her eyes. "This is Imani," she said, "our new lead singer I texted you about."

"You didn't tell me she was stunning," Casey said. "They said it was your voice that was beautiful, but now I see that it's everything about you."

Again, I looked for someone to orient me. What was happening?

When I looked back at him, he was staring intently into my eyes. His own eyes were big and dark brown, and he had surprisingly long lashes. He was actually kind of cute. My face felt warm. Was I blushing? I was totally blushing, but I'm dark enough that they wouldn't know. Or would they?

Danielle snapped her fingers in front of Casey's face. "Can we focus, Case?" she asked. "We need to decide our band name by the end of dinner."

"How about 'Blinded by Beauty'?" Casey asked, still looking at me.

I could feel my heart beating in my throat. This kind of attention was a totally new experience for me. Did I like it? Did I hate it? Was I going to throw up?

"Okay," Sarita said. "Imani, meet Casey. A little extra, but a great bass player."

Casey pulled out a notebook and began rummaging around in his backpack.

"Case, what are you doing?" Danielle asked. "You need to eat dinner so we can get to work for this audition."

"I'm following my inspiration," he said. "'Blinded by Beauty' isn't the name for the band—it's the name for my next song."

He found a pen and began scribbling.

“He’s also our songwriter,” Sarita said to me. “Who likes to write whenever inspiration strikes. Apparently, your beauty is his latest muse. Obviously, we’ll have to figure out the band name without him.”

They didn’t think this was a big deal? Was he going to be like this the whole time? Did he actually like me?

I shook my head to clear it. I was a spy. The mystery of this boy wasn’t my mission; Danielle was. I needed to focus.

After a lively discussion, we four girls decided on “Flex Five,” and Danielle wrote it on the application paper. As we walked out, Danielle looked back at Casey. “Meet us at the rehearsal classroom in ten minutes, Mr. Inspiration,” she said. “Or we might replace you as our bass player, too.”

Casey looked up at me and gave me an amazing smile. “Make it fifteen minutes,” he said to Danielle, and went back to scribbling in his notebook.

FOUR

My phone buzzed. It was my mom, sending a casual "How's it going, honey?" text. But I knew it meant that she was looking for a status update.

I was grateful to have something to ground me in my mission.

"Good," I wrote back to Mom. "Really good. I got into the band."

"I love it," Mom responded. "Day one without a hitch."

"I haven't gotten to know the other band members much yet," I wrote, trying to give her some information about where things stood without saying anything outright.

"I'm sure you'll connect soon!" wrote Mom. And I resolved to find a time to talk to Danielle alone. I put the phone away and made small talk with the girls in the band as we got set up for rehearsal. And in the back of my mind, I tried to get a grip on how I felt about this Casey situation.

I was not used to attention from boys. Once, in elementary school in DC, I had liked a boy named Rakeem and he had liked me back. But starting in middle school, everything had been different. I used to go to a mostly white school where I was considered too big to be pretty, so I'd always assumed that boys weren't interested in me. Then I switched to a school that was in a neighborhood where I got catcalled in the hallways and sexually harassed on the street. It was like whiplash. I had hated being invisible in my old school, but being visible wasn't so great, either. Now I was homeschooled and didn't have to deal with any of that.

But Casey saying he was blinded by my beauty? It wasn't being ignored and it wasn't catcalling. But it wasn't like he actually knew me. It felt . . . I don't know how it felt. Weird. Maybe it could be good? He was cute. Not as cute as Dexter, the one guy who maybe could have been my boyfriend, before our Factory jobs got in the way. I still thought about Dexter a lot. But if I wasn't really going to be able to see him again, maybe it wasn't wrong to think about Casey . . .

Five minutes later, Casey sauntered into the classroom, wearing shades. His bass guitar was slung over his back in a soft case.

He walked up to me with his hand out. "Allow me to properly introduce myself," he said. "Casey. No longer blinded by your beauty; I was prepared this time. I look forward to having a productive time being in a band with you."

Then he shook my hand vigorously.

"Imani," I managed to say. Otherwise, I was speechless. I felt a little disoriented.

He took the shades off and squinted at me, as if I were a bright light. Then blinked a few times, like his eyes were adjusting, and turned to unpack his bass.

"Excellent," Noelani said. "Now that we have a more *professional* environment, we can get to work."

"Let's warm up," Sarita said. "You like Anasuya Blackwell, right? We do a cover of her 'California Steamin.' Do you know that one?"

"Definitely," I said. Her rage anthem about West Coast fires and heat waves had been a big hit the summer before.

"Great!" Danielle said. "Let's get it."

Sarita started off with the guitar lick, and the others joined in. I took a deep breath and sang:

"All the leaves are brown
Curling like houses and burning down
All the skies are red
We want fresh air but we wear masks instead
Now is the time to stand and fight

We're not yet doomed to this plight
Time to change all the rules
Time to divest from the fossil fuels"

It wasn't just Anasuya's soaring melody; it was also the hope of the song. So many kids of my generation had given up and just talked about growing up at the end of the world. But what if that wasn't true? What if we could work together to make a new kind of world, one where we stopped destroying the planet and changed our ways?

I tried to focus on the message instead of wondering if my voice sounded good or not. I tried to put all the longing I had for a better world into my singing—like I'd heard gospel singers say, to let the spirit of the music flow through me.

After the song, I finally opened my eyes. The band was grinning at me.

"We seriously have a chance for this audition," Sarita said.

"I told you," Noelani said. "She can really sing."

"But we need an *original* song," Danielle said.

"We had a whole set list," Casey said.

"Yeah," Sarita said. "But those are all love songs about girls."

"Imani can still sing them," Casey said. "You of all girls should know that."

"We haven't even asked Imani if she would feel comfortable with that," Danielle said.

Were they asking about my sexual orientation? I hadn't discussed that as part of my cover. What should I say?

"It doesn't matter," Sarita said, shaking her head. "We're not going to get into the contest with a queer anthem."

"That part," Noelani said. "The bands that win are always more mainstream."

"Okay, fine," Casey said. "Change the lyrics. We can make it about boys."

"Who says to a guy that they love the sparkles of the sun on his hair?" Danielle asked.

"I would love it if a girl said that to me," Casey said.

No one was asking me what I thought, so I just looked back and forth as they figured out what I should sing.

"Why don't we make it a love song about music?" Danielle asked. She flipped through a stapled stack of papers.

"'Lifeline to My Heart'!" Noelani said. "That could totally be about music." She turned to Casey. "Can you work on the lyrics?"

"I need to be inspired," he complained. "I love music, but that's an ongoing thing. It's not the same as when you're really feeling someone."

Casey was looking at me. Wait. Was the flirting thing back on now?

"I can work on the lyrics," I said, partly just to change the subject. Then I had a brainstorm. "But maybe . . . I don't know . . . Danielle, could we talk it through together? I'd like to hear what you had in mind."

"Sounds good," she said.

"We should work on changing the key of the song," Sarita said. "Imani's voice is probably two steps up."

"Then we need to work in separate rooms," Danielle said. "Or you'll distract us."

"Okay," Sarita said. "Come back in, like, half an hour, and we'll see if the key is right."

"Cool," Danielle said. "And, Casey, I might need you to sing some harmonies with Imani."

Casey grinned at me. "I'm gonna enjoy this rehearsal," he said, and he started playing basslines. He was good.

"Show-off!" Danielle yelled as we left. I could hear a muffled version of his basslines until we went into a room down the hall and closed the door.

"He is so extra all the time," she said.

"Yeah," I said. "That flirty stuff is a little much."

"Oh, no," she said. "That's real. He actually likes you. I can tell."

"Really?" I said. It was so weird. Part of me was flattered, but part of me was mortified.

"Yeah," she said. "When he didn't get a big reaction from you, he toned it down. But I've known him a long time. He doesn't get all over-the-top like that unless he's really feeling someone. But it's a good thing that it's not mutual."

I nodded, but inside I was asking myself, *Is it mutual?* I mean, he was pretty cute. And a great bass player. Did I like him back? Or were those feelings just a response to having someone come at me with so much intensity?

"Noelani and Sarita are pretty chill," Danielle said. "But they've been together since the beginning of last year. And every now and then, they get on each other's nerves and the whole band feels it. Meanwhile, there's nothing chill about how Casey does relationships. I don't think the band could handle him being in a couple."

She didn't have to worry about that. I had never been in an official couple, and now was not the time to start. I was on an assignment, and my assignment was Danielle.

"Not an issue," I said. "I'm here for the music. And today I'm here to work on these lyrics. Should we get to it?"

"Definitely," Danielle said.

FIVE

Danielle was right about the song: it was about a girl, but it could also be about music. I thought about a song my parents liked, India.Arie's "Always in My Head." She sings about someone always being in her head, and the someone was music.

I turned to Casey's lyrics, which were a bit more intense. Not surprising, coming from him. *My heart pumps thoughts of you through my veins.*

I skimmed through it. "Yeah," I said. "This is definitely gonna work." A line at the end of the first verse was easy to change. *When I step in the room, you're all that I see / could this momentous force also draw you to me?*

I used a pencil to edit:

When I step in the room, you're all that I ~~see~~ hear / ~~could this~~ you're a momentous force ~~also~~ that's drawing me near ~~you to me~~.

A few lines were easy like that. But then I looked up at Danielle.

"Some parts of it are harder to change," I said. "Like where he says, *'Your presence fills me with bliss / can't wait for our first kiss.'*"

"Yeah," Danielle said. "You can't really kiss music."

I was looking for an opening, a chance to make it more personal.

"I don't know, though," I said. "Maybe what's missing is the *intensity* that people feel about music. Like, for me, when things are really bad at home, music is my salvation."

"Yes!" Danielle said. "It just allows you to tune everything out."

"Right!" I said. I hoped she would say more, but she didn't, so I went on. "So what else rhymes with 'bliss'? 'Dismiss'? That's kind of like 'tune out.'"

"The rhyme is good," Danielle said, "but the meaning isn't right. When my mom and I fight, it's not so much that music helps me dismiss her; it's like a bubble that insulates me from it."

"Perfect," I said. *"Your presence fills me with bliss / and when things are bad at home, nothing insulates me like this."*

"That's good!" Danielle said.

I wanted to ask her more about the fighting at home, but Casey stuck his head in the door. "Noelani and Sarita are just finishing up, but I'm ready to give the new key a try," he said.

"Roger that," Danielle said. "Imani did a great job with your lyrics."

"A triple threat," Casey said. "Voice, lyrics, and looks."

I decided to try to take it in stride. If Casey was going to flirt with me, I couldn't be blushing all the time. I needed to act like, yeah, cute boys compliment me all the time. Whatever. No biggie.

"Quadruple threat," I said. "I can dance, too."

Casey started to say something, but Danielle cut him off.

"We're supposed to be singing, Case," she said.

"Right," he said. "Okay, here's the new key."

Casey began to sing. I could see why the band had wanted to recruit me. His voice was on key, but not particularly strong or soulful.

"Does the new key sound right for your voice?" Danielle asked.

"I think so," I said.

"Let's go line by line," Casey suggested.

"Gimme your phone," Danielle said. "And I'll record it."

We did it as a call-and-response. He sang the

original, and I sang our revised version back to him.

"*When I step in the room, you're all that I see,*" he sang.

"*When I step in the room, you're all that I hear,*" I sang back.

"*Could this momentous force also draw you to me?*" he sang.

"*You're a momentous force that's drawing me near,*" I sang back.

I sang the next two lines back to him verbatim:

"*It's a constant obsession I can't quite explain / My heart pumps thoughts of you through my veins.*"

I had never sung with someone else like this. There was an intensity between us, like in musicals when the two leads are professing their love for each other, even though I was staring down instead of at Casey. Still, I could feel him looking at me, even as my eyes stayed glued to the revised words on my paper.

Eventually, we got to the changed lines in the second verse:

"*Your presence fills me with bliss,*" he and I sang back and forth to each other.

"*I can't wait for our first kiss,*" he sang.

I could feel myself blushing a little as I heard the line.

"*And when things are bad at home, nothing insulates me like this,*" I sang back to him, my throat a little tight.

And then we sang the final lines of the chorus back and forth:

> *"You're strong with the power to grip my heart /*
> *I long every hour that we're apart. / In a world*
> *filled with strife / I need you in my life."*

The two of us just stood there for a second, as the final notes reverberated in the air.

"Nice job," Danielle said, handing me back my phone. "Can you memorize it before we go on tomorrow?"

"Yeah," I said.

"Good," Danielle said. "We need to be prepared for this audition. Because we are going to get into this camp."

"Are you referring to the terrible bass-string episode of 2023?" Casey asked.

"We agreed never again to speak of that dark day," Danielle said. "Just get your stuff."

The three of us walked back into the other classroom. I avoided Casey's eyes and instead looked out the window at a squirrel running across the schoolyard, its long-tailed body undulating like a wave.

When we went back into our rehearsal room, Noelani and Sarita were looking at one of their phones, watching videos of the bands who made it to the finals during the previous years. The five of us crowded around the tiny screen.

Watching the other bands, I could see what they meant about mainstream. Everybody looked like they could already be a pop star. I was definitely the most full-figured lead singer I saw. I started to feel self-conscious, but then I reminded myself that I didn't need to actually win this contest—I just needed to get more connected to Danielle. Who knew? Maybe if the band lost, she'd be even more likely to confide in me than if we won.

We ran through the song with just guitar first.

"Sounds good!" Noelani said. She looked at her watch. "We have to head back to the hotel, but tomorrow we should be ready to try it with the whole band."

The hotel was about a fifteen-minute walk away, so the organizers locked up all our instruments at the school and sent us on our way. The streets of San Diego were quiet as we walked from a residential neighborhood to an area with a few businesses.

The whole time, Danielle talked nonstop about the competition and what we needed to do to win.

I didn't quite know how to insert myself into the conversation. It reminded me of when I started at the Penfield Academy in tenth grade. I didn't know anyone, and they seemed to already have their friend groups.

But I wasn't a tenth grader anymore. I was heading into my junior year, and I was a spy. I was determined to connect to this group and particularly to Danielle. The Factory depended on it.

I started listening to her more closely. It felt like a game of jump rope, watching the rope go up and down and planning when I was gonna jump in. But when we passed a vintage store called Hello Yesterday, Sarita started singing the Beatles song, changing the lyrics:

"Yesterday, this competition seemed so far away
Now I hope our band can really slay . . ."

Danielle had stopped talking to listen, and now she jumped in: *"We need to win to get away . . ."*

Everyone was laughing.

"No, guys," Noelani said. "Wrong yesterday song."

She began singing Boyz II Men's "It's So Hard to Say Goodbye to Yesterday."

"How do we get to win this competition?
This good song could be the plan to win the round
If we get to go to summer camp, I hope it's worth
all the pain
It's so hard to win—"

Sarita jumped in. "No, no! I've got it," she said, and began to sing the final line:

"It's so hard to be the next teen sensation."

"Yes!" Casey said.

"Okay, okay," Danielle said. "Casey, you get the bassline."

And then Danielle was giving us each the harmony parts. She started singing lead, with the rest of us backing her up.

"How do we get to win this competition?
This good song could be the plan to win the
round . . ."

A woman was walking her dog on the other side of the street, and she stopped to listen.

"If we get to go to summer camp, I hope it's worth
all the pain
It's so hard to be the next teen sensation."

"Bravo," the woman said, and Sarita giggled.

Danielle continued the song. She was freestyling now.

"And I'll take with me the nervousness that
plagues me when I'm onstaaaaaaage . . ."

She sang all the gospel flourishes. It was amazing.

Then all five of us jumped in on the five-part harmony.

"It's so hard to be the next teen sensation."

Then we turned a corner and saw the hotel. And just like that, Danielle clammed up.

"That was amazing," I said.

"Definitely," Sarita said as we walked into the hotel. "We need to layer in more harmonies to our audition song. Not just Imani and Casey."

"Like, I was thinking"—and Noelani began to sing—*"You're all—"*

Danielle cut her off. "Not here," she said. "Wait till we get to the room."

It was as if a switch had been flipped. Danielle was so open when we were alone. Or when there was just one lady with a dog. But in the busy hotel lobby, she became so guarded.

Maybe she had a point. There were lots of other contestants around. I recognized a couple of the guys from the suburban band I auditioned for. Plus the girl with the grills and one of the hip-hop guys.

The other band members had all arrived early enough to check in, but I still needed to get my room. Casey said good night and headed straight upstairs. Apparently, he was staying with a cousin and had a curfew.

Danielle cut her eyes at his retreating figure. "Some people snuck away from the chaperones on the eighth-grade trip to DC, and now his mom insists that he be supervised by a family member whenever he's in a big city."

I watched Casey swagger to the elevator. Not just bass player but official bad boy.

"We'll wait for you," Noelani said to me.

I got my room key, and the four of us girls headed up to the fourth floor.

And then, when we got into the elevator, it was as if a switch had been flipped again.

"I love elevator acoustics," Danielle said. "Ready? One, two, three!"

We all sang, *"It's so hard to be the next teen sensation."*

Danielle held the final note, and it reverberated in the small box.

The elevator doors opened, and we walked out like nothing had happened. Except all of us were smiling, and Sarita's giggle rang out in the hallway.

Danielle, Sarita, and Noelani were sharing a room. I was on the same floor, only a couple of doors away (probably the Factory's doing). I wasn't sure where Casey's room was.

"I just feel so lucky to have linked up with you all," I said as we all flopped on the girls' beds. "I didn't know what to expect when I came to the audition. I hoped for a cool band, but you never know."

"Are you kidding?" Noelani said. "We're the lucky ones."

"Although, I swear," Sarita said to Danielle, "I'm gonna secretly record you one of these days and submit it to *The Voice* or something."

"You better not," Danielle said, and hit her with a pillow.

It probably would have become a pillow fight, but there was a knock at the door.

"Room check," an adult voice said.

Sarita opened the door and a youngish brunette woman walked in. She had on a red T-shirt that said THE NEXT TEEN SENSATION.

"Any opposite-sex participants in this room?" she asked.

"Nope," Noelani said. She shot a glance at Sarita, and I could see them stifling smiles. Clearly, they found the heteronormative rules to be hilarious.

The woman peeked into the open bathroom door and looked in the closet. Then she consulted her clipboard.

"There are only supposed to be three of you in here," she said.

"Oh," I said. "I'm down the hall in four twenty-one."

"Kennedy, Imani," she read off her clipboard. "You need to be in your room for lights-out."

"Sure," I said. "Sorry."

"It's fine," she said. "I'll walk you over."

Noelani jumped up and hugged me.

"See you in the morning!"

Sarita hugged me, too. "Welcome to the band," she said.

Danielle stood up, but before she could hug me, the woman was ushering me toward the door. "You can pick this up in the morning, girls."

And the next thing I knew, I was sitting alone in my hotel room, suddenly exhausted, realizing I was still on East Coast time.

I barely had time to brush my teeth before I crashed.

SIX

Because of my jet lag, I was one of the first ones down at the complimentary breakfast. I had already checked in with my Factory team and let them know that so far Danielle seemed stable but that we hadn't had much of a chance to talk. Now I was eating granola and memorizing the song lyrics.

Team Hawaii, aka the rest of Flex Five, was the last to arrive downstairs. They had jet lag in the other direction—Hawaii time was three hours earlier. The crew barely made it in time to grab a few of the last egg sandwiches and some smoothies before the hotel shut down breakfast. Everyone looked bleary-eyed, except for Sarita, who had gotten up early to go jogging. The rest of them ate their food in a semi-zombie state as we walked. But Sarita sipped her green juice and chatted with me, apparently full of endorphins.

Once again, I couldn't figure out any way to engage Danielle.

After we arrived at the school, we spent forty minutes running through the song with just the guitar. We worked on expanding from two-part to five-part harmony, then decided to try it with the full band and amplification.

Danielle began bossing us around.

"Sarita, can you test that amp?" she asked. "I really want to hear it in the monitors."

Noelani was already behind the drum kit, and Danielle had her keyboard set up. Sarita plugged in the amp and tested the guitar. The chord was loud, and Danielle turned it down.

I put in the hearing protection I had brought. The Factory had given me industrial-strength earplugs. A spy can't afford to have her hearing compromised.

Casey plugged in and sound-checked the bass. Danielle took a few minutes to get the mix right.

"Imani," she ordered, "test again?"

"Check one, two," I said.

"No," Danielle said. "Sing a line."

Suddenly, I felt shy and awkward. It was one thing to just sing, but another to sing into a live microphone.

"When I step in the room, you're all that I—" I began.

"That's good," she said, interrupting me.

I felt off-kilter. I took deep breaths as she finished balancing the levels.

"Okay," Danielle said. "Let's get this rehearsal started. One! Two! Three!"

Sarita opened with a guitar lick, and Noelani started on the drums. Then both Danielle and Casey came in with the keyboard and bass. It was a smooth opening, and they had obviously rehearsed this part many times.

They went through the intro, and I opened my mouth to sing the first line.

But Casey began to sing: *"When I step in the room, you're all that I see . . ."*

Everyone stopped playing.

"Casey," Danielle said, "Imani's singing lead, remember?"

"Sorry," he said, shaking his head. "Autopilot."

All the stopping and starting and the mic and Danielle bossing me around was making me jumpy.

"Let's take it again," Danielle said. "One! Two! Three!"

I closed my eyes and tried to ground myself as the song started up.

"*When I step in the room, you're all that I hear,*" I sang. But it wasn't right. I had practiced and practiced since yesterday. I had gone over the lyrics a hundred times. But it was different with the full amplified band.

"Stop!" Danielle shouted over the music.

"I'm really sorry, y'all," I said. "I don't know what's going on."

"Let's all sing it through," Noelani suggested. "Let's have everyone sing every single line. We can play with vocal harmonies a little more. Just get us all more connected to the song."

When I step in the room . . . I was singing from the first-person perspective, from the "I," but with all of us singing together, it felt more like a "we." Noelani was right. Singing as a group really did make me feel more connected and grounded. Casey and Danielle sang some great new harmony lines, and the song seemed to come alive.

"Nice job, everyone," Noelani said.

"Okay," Danielle said. "Let's take it again. One! Two! Three!"

I kept breathing deeply as the song started up.

"*When I step in the room, you're all that I hear,*" I sang. It didn't feel so awkward. I could feel the rest of the band with me, and I made it through the whole song feeling much less self-conscious.

"That was great!" Noelani said.

"I wouldn't call it great," Danielle said. "Maybe I'd say it's an improvement. But we need to get everything tighter for this audition. Let's take it again. One! Two! Three!"

And we did it again. And again. And again. By the end of the rehearsal, not only did I not feel in *love* with music but I wasn't so sure I even *liked* music anymore. But the song was much tighter. And I had held my own. I even tried a few flourishes that sounded great.

"Tone down the gospel," Danielle said. "Remember, it's pop music."

I nodded and sang it one last time, trying to channel my inner pop star.

After four hours of rehearsal, I got a chance to rest my voice as we headed to costume and makeup.

Casey went into the guys' dressing room, and I peeked over his shoulder. It looked like they weren't getting much of a makeover, just a few accessories and a little fussing with their hair. Great.

But when we stepped into the women's dressing room, it was a totally different story. There were racks and racks of clothing and two long rows of chairs at lighted makeup mirrors. In front of the chairs was row after row of makeup, and at the far wall was another whole line of chairs for major hair transformation.

The costume fitter took us one by one. She was a rail-thin older lady, with a dyed black mane and dark eyeliner.

She began appraising Danielle, who had a tall, athletic frame.

"Size six, I think," the costume fitter said, and pointed Danielle to a rack under the windows.

Noelani was short and square-hipped. "Eight?" the woman suggested.

"I prefer my own clothes," Noelani said. She had a tomboy style and was wearing jeans and a baggy T-shirt that day.

The woman sighed. "Then at least accessorize."

Noelani shrugged and followed the woman's bejeweled finger, pointing toward the accessories.

The costumer appraised Sarita as a "ten." She pointed her to the "larger sizes," with just a touch of shade.

When she turned to me, the woman's face puckered in distaste.

"Hmmm . . ." she said, looking me over. I opened my mouth to tell her I didn't need a costume, but she cut me off, walking behind me and looking at my butt. "Definitely plus-size."

She waved me toward the far end of the room. In a dimly lit corner, there were two racks of clothes simply labeled PLUS. There, clothing from size twelve to twenty-four was all thrown together, in no particular order. Everything was sort of awful, like what someone's grandma might wear to a funeral. And I guessed anyone bigger than a size twenty-four was just completely out of luck.

My belly burned with indignation. But fortunately, I had come prepared. Mom and I had gone to a specialty plus-size store in Georgia to find a jumpsuit. She had to take it in several inches at the waist, but then it looked great. It had a shiny finish and a slight sparkle. I pulled it triumphantly out of my backpack and went in search of shoes to match.

So many of the women's shoes were super high and had tiny stiletto heels. Some were sandals that seemed to hang on to your feet with a couple straps and a lot of luck. Who could walk in something like that, let alone dance around on a stage?

There were even fewer choices in the size eleven-plus shoes. But then I saw a relatively large pair of platform black boots, with a wide heel. They were a size ten and a half, and I was an eleven, but I could make it work for one song.

I caught up with Danielle by the hair area.

"What are you doing with your hair?" I asked, looking at her four braids.

"I washed and braided it last night," she said. "The braids will make it wave."

She started to take them out and, sure enough, her hair cascaded down to her shoulders in bouncy waves.

Beside me, several hairdressers stood by. "Do you want yours flat-ironed?" one of them asked me. *Did I?* I had never pressed it before, and I wasn't sure.

"Um . . . what are my options?" I asked.

One of the women stepped forward. She was young and maybe Latina, with long blond hair. "I mean . . ." the woman began, looking over my three dozen cornrows. "If I don't flat-iron it, you could leave it as is. Or you could take it out and go for volume."

"Like an Afro?" I asked.

"Something like that," she said.

I didn't know what the next few days would hold. I had cornrowed my hair in small braids so it would last till the mission was over. If I took it out, how would I take care of it? I didn't have time to fuss with it while I was undercover.

"Um . . . are those my only options?" I asked.

"You could wear a wig," she offered.

I lit up. "Yes, please."

"You want long or short?" she asked.

"Long," Danielle said without even asking me. "Definitely. We want pop diva."

"No problem," the woman said.

Five minutes later, I looked in the mirror, the long honey-brown wig dangling down way past my shoulders. I guess the hairdresser was going for a Beyoncé look.

It was so strange seeing myself with the wig on. It wasn't just that the hair was so long—it was also that it was light brown, and it swooped back from my forehead, partially obscuring the top quarter of my face.

I had never worn anything like this. My own hair never grew past my shoulders. I kept it in cornrows: sometimes up into tight spirals on the crown of my head, sometimes in diagonals across. Or I put it in Bantu knots. Or pulled it back into a big Afro puff. I had worn it in multiple puffs or braids with beads or barrettes when I was a kid, but I'd never straightened it or worn a weave. When I was little, I sometimes told my mom I wanted long hair. She said that if I wanted it long, I could grow locs. Basically, that's when you don't comb your hair and it coils together over time and makes its own natural extensions. But I'd never done that. I hadn't been interested when I was in elementary or middle school, and it wasn't a good idea to have locs as a spy, because it's just not versatile enough. It would be hard to get them under a straight wig.

I stared at my reflection in the Beyoncé hair. Did I like it? That was the thing. I sort of hated it, because it looked so strange and foreign. But I also sort of loved it. I felt appealing in a way that was like . . .

I couldn't even say the words aloud in my head. I felt like I was whispering to myself. *Whiter.* I looked whiter. Less Black. Less African. But also, *more* Black in a certain way. More mainstream. More like other Black girls in the US. And part of me hated it. But part of me loved it.

I pulled the wig off my head. After wearing it, my own hair looked . . . less? Not enough?

"You don't like it?" the hairdresser asked.

"No," I said. "I feel too weird. Too *not me*."

"Of course it's not you," she said. "It's a wig."

"Can we get one that's my regular hair color?" I asked. Maybe that would be better.

Danielle piped up. "No," she said flatly. "Not glamorous enough. You want something that's pop-diva style. It needs to actually *pop*."

I cast around for a solution. "What about blue?"

The hairdresser grinned. "I can see it," she said. "Or maybe, like, a turquoise?"

"Yeah," I said. "Or even more blue?"

She pulled out the same style of wig in a bright royal blue. "This color?"

I held it out in front of me. I was a spy. I disguised myself all the time. Why did this feel so different?

I looked in the mirror and recalled sitting with my mom once before a mission where she wore a long wig. Both of us had medium-brown skin with hair and eyes that were nearly black. Her hair was longer than mine, pulled up in a bun. Mine was cornrowed back into short braids that hung down a few inches at the nape of my neck.

"You're beautiful," Mom had said. "With or without any type of special beauty products. It's just who you are."

"I know, Mom," I said. "But nobody looks like me. I mean, when I'm around other people my age, it makes me feel weird sometimes. A lot of the time."

Mom nodded. "But you're a spy," she said. "Even if you disguise yourself to fit in, you're never really going to be like everyone else."

In the dressing area at the audition, I looked at the wig. The thing was like a cartoon. Nobody would ever think it was my natural hair. I took a breath and put it on.

Looking at myself, I laughed out loud. It was totally glamorous. Totally pop star. Totally ridiculous. And totally not me, but I somehow managed to pull it off.

"It's perfect," I said.

And then Danielle and I started laughing, and neither of us could stop for what seemed like forever.

SEVEN

With the hair issue solved, we all headed back into the dressing-room area to reapply lipstick and put on our costumes.

"Do we just change right here?" I asked.

"I don't really care," Danielle said. She pulled her shirt off over her head. "I'm so used to this from soccer."

I was definitely not used to it. But I was slowly getting more comfortable with my body. I decided to use the fake-it-till-you-make-it approach. I stood up tall and proud as I yanked off my shirt and leggings. I tossed them into my bag and pulled out the jumpsuit. Then I stepped into it, boldly. Like I just changed every day in front of other people, putting on brightly colored skintight shiny outfits.

"Love the style," Sarita said.

"Yes," Noelani agreed. "It's giving pop star realness."

I laughed. "That's what I was going for."

Noelani had upgraded her tomboy look to include a sparkly silver vest over her black T-shirt and jeans.

Danielle had on a long black dress, slit up the side, and gold sandals.

Sarita had on a bright blue A-line dress with wide fishnet stockings and red high-heeled Mary Janes.

"Wow," Danielle said as we looked at ourselves in the mirror. "We really look like pop stars."

"Wait for it . . ." I said. Then I leaned over and put on the blue wig. I swooped my head back, and the long waves fell into place.

Yes. There were gasps.

"This outfit is crushing it!" Sarita said.

"I like your real hair better," Noelani said. "But for this costume, it's perfect."

"Hold on to your heart," Noelani said as we went to meet up with Casey and to do our last run-throughs before the actual competition.

We walked into the practice room, and for the first time ever, Casey did seem to actually be speechless. He just stood there and sort of gaped at me. I was a lot taller than him in the heels.

It felt exciting and glamorous. I knew I was supposed to be a spy above all else, but there was something so new about being considered beautiful. About having a cute guy notice me like this, not being, like, creepy or talking about my body out on the street. Like he respected my voice but also noticed my looks.

"Calm down, everyone," Danielle said as Casey gawked. "We've established that our lead singer is looking good. Can we please work on the song? We need to see what it's like to play in heels and tight clothes and everything."

"Roger that," Sarita said.

I looked around. For Danielle and Noelani, it wasn't that much of a change. They both sat down to play their instruments. Casey didn't look that different, either.

But for me and Sarita, the lead singer and guitarist, we had to get used to doing the song in high heels.

Everyone got their instruments, and we stepped into place.

"Okay," Danielle said. "Let's do this. One! Two! Three!"

I had to stop during the first take because my hair was flying around. I was turning my head swiftly, like I always did. But this time, I got a mouthful of synthetic blue strands when I went to sing the next line.

I tried to sing and spit it out at the same time.

"Stop!" Danielle said. "Imani, do you need a minute?"

"No," I said through a mouthful of hair. I put the

mic on the stand and used both hands to get my hair out of my face. "I just need to remember not to turn my head so quickly."

"From the top," Danielle said. "One! Two! Three!"

We did the song a half dozen times. By the end, my feet were killing me, and I was way too hot in the jumpsuit. But we looked and sounded like a pop band.

Which was good, because the audition was in two hours.

At five p.m., our crew walked into the dinner line, and Danielle turned to me.

"No sugar or milk," she commanded. "It'll coat your throat."

Wow, Casey wasn't the only one in this band who was intense.

"You nervous?" Noelani asked, coming up behind me.

"Not really," I said. But actually, I was. I just had to keep remembering that it wasn't my job to pass this audition. It was my job to do my best and to pretend to be invested. I was here to assess Danielle. I couldn't really draw a conclusion yet. She seemed edgy, but we were in the heat of competition. Was she always like this? Was this as edgy as she got? I really hoped that, whether we made it or not, I would have more time to talk to her and get a better sense of how much of a threat she posed to the Factory.

• • •

The five of us headed to the music building for the audition. Even with lots of other young musicians around, I felt insanely conspicuous in my purple jumpsuit and glittery eye shadow. And that was without the wig! Casey and Sarita were carrying their instruments, but Danielle and Noelani had been assured that there would be a keyboard and drum kit available in the studio.

Inside, we were met by a young blond woman with a clipboard. She checked us in and told us to have a seat. Each group was getting called into the inner studio one by one. We couldn't hear the performances, but we looked around and began to size up the waiting competition. There were lots of white groups, some Asian groups, and a few Black groups. We were by far the most diverse—three Black members, one South Asian, one Native Hawaiian.

I could see that our style was by no means over-the-top. There was lots of big hair, face sparkles, and heavy makeup. All these kids seemed ready for their fifteen minutes of fame.

In the buzz of energy that was the waiting room, I couldn't help feeling excited. I wanted to make the cut. I wanted it beyond my assignment with Danielle. Maybe I was more competitive than I thought. Or maybe I was realizing that if we made it, I would get to keep singing. And something about our song was true: music was an amazing part of life.

• • •

An hour later, it was nearly our turn. I slipped my feet back into the boots. The heels were so uncomfortable, I wasn't going to wear them any longer than necessary.

Danielle was sitting on a chair practicing, her fingers moving on a ghost keyboard. Sarita and Noelani were chanting some sort of mantra. And Casey was leaning against the wall with his eyes closed. I didn't really know what to do. I just stood there in my blue wig with my heart jackhammering in my chest. I tried to take deep breaths.

"Flex Five?" the stage manager woman called.

I blinked. "Yes!" I said, my taut voice cracking. Ugh. Perfect.

The group rallied and followed her through the door.

The inner studio was smaller than I expected. Just room enough for our group, the drum kit and keyboard set up as promised.

Across from the bandstand, three adults sat at a table. Two white guys and a woman who might have been Latina or Arab.

Sarita and Casey plugged in their instruments and did a quick check. We all tested the mic levels, and a guy at a board adjusted them till they seemed right. Then Danielle marched up to the vocal mic.

"Good afternoon!" she chirped. "We're Flex Five

from Hawaii, and we're doing the original song 'Lifeline to My Heart.'"

Then she turned sharply and strode over to the keyboard.

I tried to emulate her confidence as I took over the mic, but my steps were a bit more tentative in the high-heeled boots.

As soon as everyone was set up at their instruments, Danielle counted us off: "One! Two! Three!"

The song started up, and I closed my eyes and tried to center myself.

You know this song.

I tried to lose myself in the familiar music. *Ignore the judges. Listen to your own words.*

I took a deep breath as my cue came up.

"*When I step in the room, you're all that I hear,*" I sang.

Yes! I could hear that my voice was strong. The band was tight. All that rehearsing was paying off.

By the time we were into the second verse, I was really feeling it.

"In a world filled with strife / I need you in my life," I sang.

But then a loud voice came through the speakers.

"Thank you, Flex Five," one of the men said.

I blinked, coming out of the zone as we stopped in a bumble of dissonant sound.

“We appreciate you coming in today,” the woman said. “We’ll be in touch.”

The blond woman with the clipboard was standing at a door opposite the one we came in.

We exited the room with far less swagger than when we entered. I struggled to hold my head up and my back straight as I made my way out in the uncomfortable high heels.

The stage manager escorted us down a hall and back out to our practice room. We gathered our things in silence. Danielle walked fast on her long legs, wheeling her keyboard quickly to the door. I tossed off the wig and kicked off the boots, then grabbed my bag and shoes. I didn’t even have time to change into my sneakers as I rushed after her in the gathering dusk. Fortunately, the school was clean and there wasn’t any gum or anything gross on the floor as I hurried to the exit in my bare feet, the others right behind me.

When we were finally outside, it was like a dam had burst in Danielle.

“What the hell?” she demanded. “They didn’t even listen to the whole song?”

“Maybe it’s a good sign,” Noelani said, rushing to keep up with her. “Maybe they knew right away that they wanted us.”

“I can’t!” Danielle said. “I can’t sit at home with my mother for the rest of the summer. Since the hurricane, we're in this small apartment and she works at home. Plus, she didn't have the money to put me in sports camp this year."

"Don't worry," Sarita said. "You can hang at my house all day."

"I wish!" Danielle said. "I'm grounded most of the time. I think she comes up with reasons to punish me. She wants to keep me under surveillance. She's afraid I'm going to go around blabbing about the family business. Mom, nobody cares about your weird culty job from when I was in middle school! I just want to move on with my life. I've got to get out of there or, I swear, it will destroy me."

Yikes—"weird culty job" felt like it was inviting questions that I didn't want her to answer! I needed to change the subject in a hurry.

We were standing on the sidewalk in front of the school now. I tried to think of what to say. But before I could open my mouth, Sarita had moved in close.

"Danielle," Sarita said. She put a finger under Danielle's chin and tilted her face up. "Look at me. You can stay with me for the rest of the summer if we don't get in. You don't have to stay home and let your mom drive you nuts."

Danielle sank into Sarita's shoulder. "Oh my God," she said, "thank you so much."

"I got you, girl," Sarita said.

"What about the rest of us?" Casey asked. "Danielle's not the only one who was affected by the hurricane."

"You'll be fine," Sarita said. "Your house lost a few trees. Her house is no longer standing."

Casey didn't get to respond because a minivan pulled up in front of us.

"I got us a rideshare back to the hotel," Casey said.

"Thank goodness," I said. I hadn't had a chance to put my sneakers on. But even more important, I was desperate to get back to the hotel, where I could check in with the Factory. "Culty job"? I needed to report that.

I opened the door and climbed into the back seat, then began eagerly pulling on my socks and sneakers. Casey came in and sat next to me. His bass took up the third place on the back seat of the van. With the big instrument, we were sitting with the sides of our legs touching. I looked out the window. If he was looking at me, it would be a little too close at this range. I suddenly felt shy.

Danielle and Sarita opened the van's rear door and put their instruments in the way back behind us.

Noelani climbed into the middle row of seats. I was glad for the third passenger. It broke up some of the awkwardness between me and Casey. And I needed to get my head back into my spy game. Danielle was volatile, and I needed to find a way to get into a one-on-one conversation with her. Or at the very least, join her conversation with Sarita.

“Are they coming, too?” the rideshare driver asked Casey, gesturing to Danielle and Sarita on the sidewalk.

Danielle was shaking her head, and Sarita had an arm around her and was murmuring in her ear.

“Go on ahead,” Sarita called to us. “Danielle needs the walk.” She put both their backpacks in the front passenger seat and closed the door.

What? Wait! I wanted to say I would walk with them, but I was jammed into the back seat. It would be too awkward.

“Okay, Booski,” Noelani said to Sarita out the window. “We’ll see you at the hotel.”

The van pulled away from the curb, and I sat there, stunned.

Damn. How did I let myself get separated from her? Danielle was my assignment. I should have stuck to her like glue.

Just before the van turned the next corner, I could see Danielle and Sarita sitting close together on the curb and putting their sneakers back on.

“Is Danielle gonna be okay?” I asked Noelani.

“I think so,” she said with a shrug. “Let’s give the besties some time together.”

I risked a sidelong glance at Casey in the seat next to me. He sat with his arms folded, his face inscrutable behind a pair of shades.

We rode to the hotel in silence. And I just had to hope that I wasn’t sitting a mile away while Danielle spilled everything to someone who was not a Factory agent.

When we got to the hotel, a dessert bar was waiting for us. Casey and Noelani went for the treats, but I hurried up to my room to check in with my team.

Ten minutes later, I was in a videoconference with my mom. I had told her about Danielle's "culty job" comment.

"How bad do you think it is?" Mom asked. "Should we pull her out?"

"I don't know," I said. "It really depends on if the band gets chosen or not. If so, I think we're fine. If not, I worry that she'll melt down."

"How soon do you find out?"

"They said they'd let us know first thing tomorrow," I said.

Mom nodded. "It's gonna be a rough night."

EIGHT

She was right. It was much harder to sleep the second night in the strange hotel room. I had been on solo missions before, and I was extra tired from the time change, but somehow I was awake for a while, thinking I might never sleep. And then abruptly, I must have knocked out.

I woke before dawn when I heard a strange noise.

My spy training kicked in. *Don't open your eyes yet. If there's an intruder, you don't want them to know you're awake. It gives you an edge if they think they're still undetected.*

I kept my eyes shut and listened.

Tap-tap-tap. Wait. It was just someone knocking on the door. But who?

I opened the door to find Danielle.

"We made the cut!" she said, striding in

triumphantly. "I could hardly sleep. I just kept going down to the lobby all night. I finally fell asleep around one and then woke up again at four and just sat there until someone came and posted it twenty minutes ago!"

"That's great!" I said. I wanted to say, *You could've just texted, instead of being so extra*, but I was trying to build a connection with her. I didn't know yet if it would be cool to joke like that or not. I was relieved to see her looking so happy, though. It felt like the threat had lessened, but I still wanted to make sure she was in a better place.

"I know!" she said. "I woke Noelani up to tell her, but she just said 'yay' and went back to sleep. Sarita always goes running in the morning. I don't know which room is Casey's."

"I'm so glad you came," I said.

"You don't understand what this means to me," she said. "I've been praying for this opportunity to get a break from my mom. It's just the two of us in that tiny temporary apartment."

"Yeah," I said. "I can imagine." This seemed like my big opportunity to get her to open up, but what should I say?

"I feel like a prisoner there, with her watching me every second," Danielle said. "But at camp, we'll finally have some freedom. Oh my God, I just can't wait!"

"Yeah," I said. "Me too." How was I going to get her to confide in me and work the conversation around to the idea of therapy?

"Wait," she said. "Is it seven yet?"

"Almost," I said, looking at my watch. "Why?"

"At seven Sarita should be back. She gets up early to go jogging because it's so hot in Hawaii later in the day. Even with the time change, her body just gets up with the sunrise."

"Wow," I said. "She got up early to jog, even after the competition?"

"Seven days a week," Danielle said. "She's like clockwork. Yes! It's six fifty-five." No, this was not good. I could never get anywhere with Danielle when Sarita was around.

"Okay," I said, improvising. "We can listen to a song first." I had to make a connection with her, find out where her head was at.

I pulled out my phone and opened the music app. I put on Deza's "Black Girl."

We each put a single earbud in our ears and lay back on the bed to listen:

Black girl, Black girl, so much to say
So many obstacles get in the way.

I was hoping that emphasizing what we had in common, both of us as Black girls, trying to express ourselves creatively, would help.

After the song was over, I gushed, "I just love Deza."

"Me too," Danielle agreed.

"Hey, let me play another—" I began.

But she interrupted me. "It's six fifty-nine! I'm just gonna call Sarita."

And then she was on her phone calling Sarita. She listened for a moment, then hung up.

"She didn't pick up?" I asked. "Want to listen to another song?"

"Maybe she's in the shower," she said. "I'll head back to our room."

"I'll go with you," I said, throwing on a pair of sweats and sliding my feet into slippers.

"Sarita seems really great," I said as we headed down the hallway.

"She and I started at our high school the same year," Danielle said. "She was my first friend."

When we got to their room, Noelani was asleep in the bed. Sarita wasn't anywhere in sight, and the bathroom door was wide open.

Danielle stepped back out into the hallway and closed the door.

"Where is she?" Danielle asked, sitting down against the wall. I sat down beside her, right next to the door.

"Like I said," Danielle continued, "I hung a lot with the girls in soccer, but Sarita was my day one. And then . . . well, when things started to get harder at home . . . I mean, the soccer crew was okay as long as we were winning, but those girls basically had everything. They had money, and they were just sort of used to me being, like, someone who would just listen to them and be, like, 'Wow! That sounds so amazing!' But when I was upset about something, they were, like, 'Let's go shopping to cheer you up!' But shopping couldn't fix it. I was supposed to be all happy and grateful. But I wasn't . . . I guess I just didn't fit in with that crowd anymore."

Yes! She was finally opening up a little.

"I know what you mean," I said. "At this one school I went to, the kids would be, like, let's go to some super-expensive restaurant or whatever. And you can't be, like, 'Uh . . . are you treating?' Everyone's supposed to be, like, 'Yeah! That's a great idea!' And if you go and order French fries, and everyone else has two mocktails and five appetizers, then everyone's throwing down their parents' platinum cards all 'Let's split it five ways!' And you're counting the singles in the bottom of your pocket!"

"Yes!" Danielle said. "I just couldn't—"

But then the elevator opened and Sarita walked out. She was wearing athletic gear, with a towel around her neck.

"Sarita!" Danielle said, leaping up and running down the hallway. "We made the cut!"

Dang, I thought. *So close.*

The two girls hugged, and I couldn't hear most of what they said as they walked back, heads together.

". . . I know . . ." Danielle was saying when they got back in earshot. "Yes! That's just what I thought. It was definitely the lucky necklace!"

"We did it!" I said.

"Yes, we did!" Danielle said. "But we can't kick back—we need to check out the competition. They'll be posting all the winners later today. We need to get online and study the other bands. Now our job is to get from the camp to the big show in Northern California."

Half an hour later, I was on with Jerrold.

"Your mother shared your observations with me," he said. "Thank you for your work on this. I was hoping we wouldn't have to take drastic action, but just the fact that she mentioned her mother's 'culty job' feels too close for comfort. We need to pull Danielle. We can do it while she's in transit."

"You mean full-on deport her from the US?" I tried to hide my dismay.

"Amani," he said, "the agent she was connected to is currently doing critical work. He's supporting some whistleblowers at a company that could make a huge difference for Black workers in the South. Now is not a time we can risk him being exposed."

My heart ached for Danielle, getting yanked away just as she had achieved her dream. "But what if there was another way?" I asked, thinking furiously.

"I'm listening," Jerrold said.

"Danielle isn't thinking about her family when she's focused on the band," I said. "Your best-case scenario was that she wasn't that upset. Well, it's clear that she *is* upset. But your second-best-case scenario is that she gets help to deal with her grief. Going to camp with Danielle is going to be a great opportunity to get closer to her. We'll probably be bunking together, and it'll be a high-pressure situation. I can try to bring up the idea of therapy then."

Jerrold frowned. "But why would she confide in you? Why not one of her other friends?"

I hesitated. The truth was, I wasn't sure that Danielle would talk to me with Sarita around. "It's true. Sarita is Danielle's go-to for everything emotional. She might block me from connecting with Danielle. I think we need to find a way to eliminate Sarita."

Jerrold did a double take on the video screen. "Amani, you realize we're a nonviolent organization, right?"

"What?" I said. "No! I don't mean to harm her in any way. Just keep her from going to camp."

Jerrold let out a sigh of relief. "I was worried for a second that our espionage training had been too hardcore," he said. "But it feels risky. I still think extracting Danielle is best."

"That's only a temporary solution, though," I said.

"We have the resources to keep her off the grid for eighteen months," he said.

"But then what?" I asked. "If you pull her out, she's going to be even angrier with her mom and with the Factory. I don't think you'll convince her to go to therapy in that case."

"True," said Jerrold, frowning.

"And with all due respect, adults always forget that their power over teens is temporary. Danielle is sixteen. She'll be eighteen in a couple of years. Then her mother will have zero legal control over anything she does. If you extract her, she'll have a story that the media will eat up. *My parents were Black spies. I got kidnapped and sent away.*"

Jerrold sighed. "You're not wrong about that. But this operation in South Carolina is critical. I'm willing to take drastic action to give us two years to defuse the bomb that is Danielle."

"I think this could solve both of your problems," I said. "Camp will give her a creative outlet, which could help all on its own. And if we remove Sarita, I think I have a good chance of connecting with her and getting her into therapy. If it doesn't work, you can always extract her later."

"I'm considering it," he said. "What did you have in mind?"

"Well, it's summer break," I said. "Sarita's parents are supportive of her doing music as a hobby, but they ultimately want her to be in a more lucrative field. Could you get her a surprise scholarship to a big STEM camp or something?"

"Maybe," Jerrold said. "But there's no guarantee Sarita would be willing to go."

"Good point," I said. "She'd have to leave her best friend and her girlfriend."

"But what if we offered her family an all-expenses-paid vacation?" Jerrold asked.

"Yeah!" I said. "That would be good . . . but they already live in Hawaii. If you send them somewhere else for a vacation, Sarita might tell them to just take her little brother and still go to the camp. It has to be something that they would insist she join." I thought for a moment. "Wait! Could you get an all-expenses-paid trip to India? I overheard Sarita saying that her parents have been wanting the kids to visit their homeland. They would totally make her go."

"I like it," Jerrold said. "A lot more expensive than a typical vacation, but it's an offer the family won't be able to refuse. I'll get our team on it."

I liked this idea, until I realized the drawback. "But won't our team get disqualified from the camp if we don't have a guitarist?" I asked.

"Maybe not," Jerrold said. "They did that speed dating with vocalists. I'll work on that, too, and get back to you." Then he gave me a hard look through the screen. "I'm willing to give this a try, but it's important that you let us know right away if you think Danielle is going to snap. There's a lot riding on this."

I nodded. I could only hope that my instincts were right on this one.

NINE

One of the weird things about being a spy is that you don't handle the little details of your own life. Like packing for a trip—the Factory team did that for me. Up until the moment that we left for camp, I was focused on the mission. So it wasn't until I was in a car with the other members of the band, headed north on Highway 101, that I truly realized I was going to sleep-away camp for the first time.

By dinnertime, we were approaching the Bay Area. Casey was riding separately, with his cousin, and Danielle, Sarita, and Noelani had all fallen asleep in the back seat. A counselor named Cassandra was driving. She was a quiet young white woman in her twenties who played the flute.

I closed my eyes but couldn't sleep. I found myself

sort of composing a new song about being a teen spy. I would never sing it aloud, even though spying was a metaphor in the song—Danielle was too smart, and I wasn't going to take any chances.

When the other girls started to wake up, I pretended that I was also just finishing a nap. Rubbing my eyes, I pulled out my phone to find a thumbs-up emoji from Jerrold. I wasn't sure what it meant, but I was glad to have some good news.

We ended up stopping at a hotel near San Jose. As we sat around the hotel room eating Thai food, Danielle talked nonstop about camp and how excited she was.

I was mostly exhausted. I begged off early, crashing. I was confident that in Danielle's high mood, she was not about to let anything slip.

The next morning, we were carrying our stuff back down to the car when Sarita got a call.

"Hi, Mom," she said as we piled into the elevator. "Yeah, we're almost to Oakland . . . What? . . . That's great!" She grinned in delight. "When?" She listened for a moment and her face fell. "What? . . . Mom, no! What about—?"

Sarita fled out of the elevator, and Noelani and Danielle rushed after her.

Sarita listened for a moment, then spoke up. "Mom, I know it's an amazing opportunity but . . . Yes, but . . . I also have an amazing opportunity at camp."

“They’re not letting you go, after all?” Noelani whispered.

Sarita shook her head.

“No, that’s not it? Or no, they’re not letting you go?” Danielle asked.

Sarita waved them both away and stepped to the other side of the room.

“Mom, that’s so unfair,” she said. “What about my bandmates?”

Danielle’s eyes widened in worry. She and Noelani flanked Sarita.

“Can’t we do it later in the year? . . . Why not?” Sarita was on the verge of tears.

Noelani put an arm around her, and Danielle held her hand on the other side.

“And I don’t get any say in this at all?” She began to cry, the tears spilling down onto her Anasuya Blackwell T-shirt.

Danielle and Noelani both looked anxious, not knowing what was happening with Sarita. Of course, I knew what was happening, but I tried to fix my face into the right amount of anxiety. Not the same as the best friend or the girlfriend, but not the unsurprised face of the spy who secretly engineered this problem behind the scenes.

When Sarita got off the phone, she shared the news with all of us: her family had gotten an unexpected dream trip to India. They would be leaving in the next few days.

“What about the band?” Danielle asked.

“That’s what I asked,” Sarita said. “But I don’t have a choice. Apparently, they have subs at the camp who can fill in.”

Half an hour later, the three of them were still crying as our driver, Cassandra, prepared to drop Sarita at the Oakland airport en route to camp.

I felt awful. The entire back seat was in tears, while Cassandra and I awkwardly kept our eyes on the road ahead. I kept reminding myself: *This is really for their own good. It’s a fantastic experience for Sarita and her family. It’ll keep Danielle from getting sent out of the country indefinitely—then they’d* really *be crying.* But that thought didn’t make me feel any better.

As the airport sign came into view, Danielle burst out, “It’s like I’m cursed. Every time something good happens, something bad happens right after. I was so excited about camp, and now it’s the worst!”

“You know what?” Noelani said. “We don’t know the future. So I say maybe there’s gonna be something amazing that happens. Maybe you’ll have an incredible adventure in India, Booski. There’s only one thing I know for sure. In a couple weeks, we’ll all be back together, and that’s all that matters.”

“You’re right,” Sarita said. “And maybe you’ll get a second guitarist and win the competition, and we’ll be one of those big deal bands with two guitarists, and it’ll be amazing.”

The two of them looked at Danielle.

But she just shook her head and started crying again.

"It's not gonna be the same without you," she said to Sarita. "How can it be good without my best friend?"

"It's true that it won't be the same," Noelani said. "It's gonna be different, but that doesn't mean that it can't also be good."

"I think it's a bad sign," Danielle said.

"Dani." Sarita took Danielle's face in her hands. "Don't spiral. Focus. I want to hear you say, 'I will be kicking ass at this camp.'"

"I can't," Danielle said.

We were turning off the freeway toward the airport.

"Yes, you can," Sarita said. "If I can leave my girlfriend, my best friend, and go to my homeland where my family will make fun of my terrible Hindi and it'll be a thousand degrees, then you can kick some ass at this camp. I want to hear you say it."

"I promise to kick ass at the camp," Danielle said, with a trace of a whine in her voice.

"Louder," Sarita said.

"I promise to kick ass at the camp," she said, a little louder.

We were driving up the ramp to the terminals.

"You promise to do what?" Sarita asked.

"Kick ass," Danielle said flatly.

"Do what?"

Danielle sighed. "Kick ass."

We pulled up to the curb at the terminal.

"Look," Sarita said, "I will parachute down from this plane if you don't tell me what you're going to do."

"Kick ass," Danielle said with a tiny hint of a smile.

"Kick what?" Sarita asked.

"KICK ASS!"

"Thank you," Sarita said. "Now I can go."

We all got out of the car, and I gave Sarita a hug goodbye. Then she hugged Danielle, and the two of them cried. She hugged Noelani, and they cried and kissed goodbye. And then she was entering the airport, and a cop was telling us we had to move the car. And then we were back on the freeway, one passenger down, and everyone in the back seat was crying again.

We drove the rest of the way to Portland under a cloud. Danielle eventually stopped crying and sank into a sullen mood, her enthusiasm totally gone. Noelani was crying quietly with her head against the window. Each of them would pull out their phones from time to time and seemed to be texting. Sometimes they would get texts at different times, and sometimes simultaneously. I assumed they were from Sarita.

I started worrying that we had done the wrong thing. I knew that losing Sarita would be a blow, but it was worse than I'd expected. Danielle had gone from bubbly to brooding, and she seemed much closer to spilling everything than before. From the front seat, I tried to watch them in the rearview mirror without them catching me. With the constant hum of the car and the surrounding traffic, it would be easy for her to confide in Noelani without me even hearing it.

But the two of them seemed to be in separate worlds of gloom. And after a while, I realized it wasn't just worry that I was feeling—it was guilt. Yes, I might be protecting the Factory. But I had also just ruined three girls' summer vacation.

TEN

When the car finally pulled up in front of the camp, it was late evening. The place was sort of what I had expected from the movies and TV shows about camp: lots of green trees and grass, with a cluster of cabins in the background. There was a group of people standing around, mostly young adults, under a banner that said WELCOME, CAMPERS!

Just as we pulled in, I got a text from Jerrold: "Be alert for an update."

"Attention, please!" a counselor yelled when our car pulled into the parking lot. "Turn off your phones and text your goodbyes. As you learned when you registered, this camp is tech-free."

What? I had never registered; the Factory had signed me up. Did they know?

"Wait!" I texted Jerrold back. "They're about to confiscate our phones."

Sure enough, when we walked into the main hall, there was a woman by the door of the rustic building taking every single device.

I waited till the last second to turn it off, but there was no reply from Jerrold before I surrendered my phone and lost all contact with my team.

First, they had us drop off our sleeping bags and luggage where we were sleeping. The cabins were cozy and slept four kids plus a counselor. Most of the bands were single gender, but there were a few mixed-gender bands. We had a girl cabin for the three of us and Cassandra, and Casey would share a cabin with a couple of guys from another mixed band. Apparently, his family trusted him not to run off if he was in the middle of nowhere.

After we had dumped our stuff, they fed us a late dinner. The dining hall was a long, wooden building with institutional tables and plastic dishes. At first, it was just girls in the dining hall. It turned out that the boys' cabins were farther away. Our crew was almost to the front of the line when the boys walked in.

Casey slid into line beside us. He looked cute, in faded jeans and an old-school hip-hop De La Soul T-shirt. Up ahead, we could see that the food was cafeteria style and predictably bland. Danielle grabbed a tray and skipped the main course. She just put several desserts on her plate and went to sit down. Noelani was a vegan, so she had to go to a special window to get her food. Casey and I stood in the line together.

"Wow," he said. "I leave you all alone for one day, and you lose the guitarist?"

"Do not bring it up with Danielle or Noelani," I said. "They're both really upset."

"I'm not pointing any fingers," Casey said. "But we never lost band members before you got here. I'm just saying."

For a moment, I was horrified. It actually *had* been me who got rid of Sarita.

"I'm just joking," he said. "You're the best thing that's ever happened to this band. You're the reason that we're even here."

"You're giving me way too much credit," I said. "You wrote the song; Danielle made us practice ten zillion times. It's a group effort."

"You're right," he said. "But I hope it's okay with you if I think you're amazing."

I gave an awkward grin. "No comment."

After everyone sat down with their food, there was an orientation, and I learned what made this camp different from many others—it was designed for musicians. There were electrical outlets in all the cabins for our amps, and while none of the buildings were soundproofed, they had designated sleeping cabins and rehearsal cabins. There were ten bands, and the rehearsal cabins were far enough apart that we couldn't hear one another.

While other kids were asking about concessions and internet access, I found my spy training kicking in: What would be the best way to escape if there was danger? What would be the best extraction point if I needed to get out quickly? And of course, I kept my eye on the adults to see where they seemed to be getting cell reception. Somehow, I would need to get my hands on a cell phone so I could report in to HQ.

There was a lot of talk about how we were at camp so they could nurture us. But as much as they tried to make it sound like an educational opportunity where we were one big happy family, it was obviously super-competitive. Camp was essentially the semifinals for a major prize.

Out of the ten bands here at camp, only one would be chosen for the big competition in Northern California. No runners-up. No consolation prizes. The chosen band would get to perform along with teen bands from all over the US. And the venue would be packed, because the bands would open for the K-pop group Sound Cake. Sound Cake would crown the winning band, and being on their social media was the equivalent of a million dollars in PR in and of itself.

The adults at camp were predominantly white. Like our driver, Cassandra, the counselors were young adults who slept in the cabins with us. The teachers were older adults who stayed at an inn nearby, but they ate meals with us.

One teacher in a black T-shirt and faded jeans got up at the front of the room. His hair was slicked back and dyed black, with just a whisper of white at the roots. I swear, it was like he was there to inspire discouragement.

"I see you all as you walk through these doors," he said. "All of you want to be—like the name of the contest—*The Next Teen Sensation*. But it's simple math. Everybody can't be number one. I've been in this industry for decades. Believe me, I can almost always pick the winners. Most of the time, I can tell in the first ten seconds if someone has what it takes. I can for sure tell in the first half a minute. It's that thing that grabs you, right here."

He put his hand on his belly. Was it his job to make everyone in the room feel insecure?

But then, with the woman who went after him, it was like they were putting on a con. Like the dyed-hair guy's job was to make us feel desperate, and her job was to tell us that the camp had all the answers.

She had short hair and jeans paired with a colorful tunic.

"You all are so fortunate," she said. "When we were paying our dues, there was no one to hold our hands and give us all the inside info. But here, at *The Next*

Teen Sensation, that's exactly our job. We know who already has what it takes. And for the rest of you, we know how to help you get it, so that you have a chance to win. If you come by star quality naturally, don't rest on your laurels. These other campers are coming for you, and hard work can trump natural talent. Everyone needs to bring their A-game."

There was only one exception to the hypercompetitive theme—the songwriting teacher. She had wild, graying hair and wore long dresses. She was probably the oldest teacher, and she looked a little like a hippie. Most of the teachers wanted us to call them by their last names, but Sally asked us to use her first name, like the counselors.

"My job is to make you reach deep inside," she said, putting both hands on her heart. "I want each of you to get in touch with your story as a way to add depth to your performances." Making us reach deep inside? Was that a promise or a threat?

Then the director came up. She was the opposite of Sally. She had her hair in a bun and wore a starched, button-down shirt with crisp slacks. She didn't look like she belonged in an outdoor location. I bet she moved from her air-conditioned office to her air-conditioned car to the air-conditioned inn where she was staying. "We hope you enjoyed yourselves," the director said. "Because from here on in, it's all work."

• • •

After dinner, Noelani was still gloomy, but all the talk about the competition had Danielle perking up.

We hiked up to the cabin with our flashlights. I had strategically gotten myself on the bottom bunk below Danielle. That way, I could easily escape if needed, and I would know if she was sneaking out.

"How about that songwriting teacher?" Noelani said. "She seems like it's her mission in life to get us all to confess or something."

I laughed along with everyone, but I had that same feeling. Considering my mission, she had me worried.

We all got into our sleeping bags, and I lay there listening to the night sounds. I heard crickets. And maybe frogs. There was the occasional hoot of an owl and the bark of a larger animal, like a coyote.

From time to time, I heard the soft swish of one of the other girls moving in her sleeping bag. But all of my bedding had been packed by the Factory. When I moved in my bed, I didn't make a single sound.

ELEVEN

At breakfast the next day, I was a bit bleary-eyed. It had taken me a long time to fall asleep. I'd never slept in a room full of other kids before, and never out in nature like this.

Obviously, I wasn't the only one who'd had a rough night. Several of the other kids were drinking coffee, including Casey and Danielle.

I found myself watching both of them, but for different reasons. Danielle was my assignment. I was supposed to track her moods, see if she was talking to anyone, listen in if I could. But there was nothing to track. She stayed quiet and ate slowly.

Casey totally ignored me. Was it as simple as him not being a morning person? He had been so warm the evening before. We had had an easy rapport. A sort of connection. But it seemed like he ran hot and cool. I didn't know where I stood with him.

As we headed out to our morning rehearsal, the teachers reminded us—especially the vocalists—to drink lots of water, even more than usual, because of the heat and the dust.

I filled up my canteen, and we trudged along the river path to the rehearsal cabin that had FLEX FIVE written on the chalkboard slate out front.

"We're really more like Flex Four," Danielle said.

"Yeah," Noelani agreed. "Do we know when our guitarist is supposed to arrive?"

"Probably sometime today," said Casey. "I think they're flying up from LA."

"Okay," I said. "Fingers crossed."

Noelani opened the door to the rehearsal cabin, and we found our keyboard and drum kit already set up. What I didn't expect, though, was a girl with bright pink hair and an electric guitar. She had her back to us and was plugging into an amp.

"Excellent!" Danielle said, and offered her first smile of the day.

"Welcome!" Noelani said.

The girl turned around, and I was speechless for a moment. She grinned and walked over to where we stood.

"Hi!" she said. "I'm your new guitarist, Andréa."

I fixed my face and said hello to my co-spy, the girl who was basically my best friend.

TWELVE

Andréa was also a Factory operative. I had met her earlier that year, during her first solo mission. The last time I saw her in person, we had just finished— Actually, never mind. I probably shouldn't share that. It's classified by the Factory. But we had been in touch since then via text.

"You're our guitarist," I said, stating the obvious.

"Yeah," she said. "I usually play folklórico guitar. But when I heard about the contest and found out I would be an alternate, I started practicing a ton. I guess I did a good job."

"Got it," I said.

"Glad you're here," Noelani said. We all introduced ourselves, then Noelani suggested that we play our song for her.

"No need," Andréa said. "They sent it to me when it

was confirmed I'd be subbing in. They didn't want you all to be at a disadvantage."

"This is the best news since we got here," Casey said.

Danielle was quiet. She didn't seem as enthused as the rest of us.

"You play folklórico?" Noelani asked. "Do you think we could add some type of Latin flair to the song?"

"I hadn't thought of that," Andréa said. "Let's see."

"I don't see any reason to change things," Danielle said. "What Sarita did was good. Let's stick to that."

"Sure," Andréa said. "Whatever you all want. I'm here for you."

Noelani led us in a vocal warm-up, and then we got down to it.

Danielle counted us off: "One! Two! Three!"

We sounded pretty good with Andréa—at least as good as we had with Sarita. Afterward, the rest of us congratulated Andréa, but Danielle still didn't look happy. She started grilling her. "Is this your first contest?"

"No," Andréa said. "I've competed in folklórico contests before."

"But it's your first *mainstream* contest?" Danielle said. "Did they brief you on the rules?"

"Just that we would be playing the song this afternoon and competing later on," Andréa said.

"This afternoon is the critique session," Danielle

said, sounding irritated that she had to explain it, even though no one had asked her to. "We play the song that got us here, they give us feedback about the strengths and weaknesses, and then we have to develop a new, original song during the camp."

"Cool," Andréa said, unfazed by Danielle talking down to her.

The five of us walked toward the dining hall, but Andréa said she had to run back to the cabin first.

"I forgot my vitamins," I said. "I'll walk you over." I turned to the rest of the crew. "Meet everyone at lunch?"

The other three nodded, and I walked with Andréa to our bunks.

We stepped into the cabin as if we were strangers. After we closed the door, I called out to our counselor. "Cassandra?"

No answer.

I saw that Andréa had put her stuff on the top of the other bunk, above Noelani.

I put a finger to my lips and peeked into the bathroom. Empty.

Andréa and I looked at each other and grinned.

"I can't believe it's you!" I said, walking over and giving her a big hug.

"I know," she said. "I'm here to help. But Danielle is obviously not my biggest fan."

"I think she's just upset that you're replacing her

best friend," I said. "She'll warm up. Do I need to brief you?"

"No," she said. "Jerrold briefed me extensively on the way here. We flew straight from the audition."

"In LA?" I asked.

She nodded. "I don't know what strings he had to pull to get me in front of them as a potential sub," she said. "I've never practiced guitar so hard in my life. I was, like, 'Yes! I gotta make this audition!'"

"I'm so impressed," I said. "I had no idea you played an instrument."

"You think that's impressive?" she asked. "Wait till you see my secret weapon."

She stood back and lifted up the bottoms of her bootcut jeans. Strapped to each of her ankles was a cell phone.

"What?" I whispered. "You are amazing!"

"Jerrold said I would need to smuggle them in," she said. "I let them confiscate a decoy."

Fortunately, I was wearing a baggy pair of jeans. I put the cell phone in the front pocket and gave her one last hug.

"Best camp ever," I said, and we walked together to the dining hall.

Having Andréa there gave me confidence. I was really hoping that I would be able to get through to Danielle, but after lunch, we went straight to the performances.

There was a small stage set against the far wall, with a drum kit, keyboards, an amp, and a monitor. The first group was a boy band with spiky hair and pouty faces.

"We're Step to This," the baby-faced lead singer announced. Then the drummer started, and the rest of the instruments fell in.

The song was catchy, in that syrupy way where your inner five-year-old loves the bouncy melody. But the lyrics were kind of insulting—like all a boy had to do to get your attention was like you.

I thought about Casey, and how intoxicating it was to be liked the way he said he liked me. It was like a wave of admiration that totally knocked me off-balance. But now he was focused on the music. Did he not like me anymore? Did I *want* it to be over? Did I want it to happen some more? Part of me was relieved, but part of me was disappointed. That intensity had been quite a buzz. Someone cute and talented thought I was beautiful.

After Step to This finished their song, the director came up to give them her critique. She was still clapping when she got onto the stage.

"As you can see," she began, "this is as compelling as any of today's current hits."

They smiled at the compliment.

"Which is a problem," the director went on. "This niche is already filled. There's nothing new here. Those bands already have a following. Vienna Smith could record herself coughing, and thousands of people would buy it. You have to do the impossible. You need to stand out while simultaneously fitting in. There has to be something different about you so that you can cut through the noise, but not so different that it doesn't fill the same appetite. Step to This needs to step it up. Boy bands need something different. Even if it's just visual. Justin Bieber had that ridiculous hair. It was impractical and silly-looking, but you couldn't forget it. What's gonna be your thing? Spiky hair? It's not working. If it's visual, it needs to be more cutting edge—something I haven't seen before. Or it needs to be substantive. Any other teachers have feedback?" A few of them did.

She didn't even ask if the campers had anything to say. I was a spy, so I wouldn't have said anything no matter what. But if I had been there as myself, I would have said something about how their song would have benefited from respecting the mind of the imaginary girl they were singing to.

THIRTEEN

Flex Five was band number seven. As we set up, Danielle sort of barked commands at us in an irritated voice. Then she counted us off. Still, I felt reassured to have Andréa by my side. I might have sung better than at the audition.

"Lovely voice," the director began, looking at me. "But I would consider having more than one lead vocalist. It's about a range of visuals. Do you also play guitar? Could the guitarist sing lead on one of your songs?"

I was a step behind. A "range of visuals"? What did that mean? I *didn't* play guitar. And why did she think that Andréa should sing lead? She didn't even ask if she could sing.

I stood there confused, until Noelani caught my eye. Her eyebrows were knit together and her jaw was tight. And then it hit me. I felt a burning in my chest. The director liked the way Andréa looked: thin and feminine. Wait. No. Not only was Andréa thin, but almost light enough to pass for white, unlike Danielle, the other thin and feminine one in our group. Was this really happening? Was she suggesting that we should pick the lead singer based on appearance?

I tried to fix my face. Not only was I trying to look "professional," but I was also a spy. You never knew what you would overhear when you were pretending to be someone else.

"You just have to figure out how to maximize your archetypes," she was saying to no one in particular. Then she zeroed in on me again. "Do you rap?" she asked. "We haven't had much in the way of rap this year. You could maybe do a verse after the bridge. You know, give it a little something extra they could use in the urban market. Teachers, any other feedback?"

The hippie songwriting teacher, Sally, spoke up. "The lyrics were passable," she said. "But the love song to music is neither new nor the type of song that cuts through the noise. Your song needs to make people *feel* something. Describing your feelings about music doesn't make other people feel things. You need something more personal. More self-revelatory. Think about it."

I was still reeling from the previous comments about "visuals" and the question about whether I rapped. I realized my breathing was shallow.

"Thank you," the director said, and called for the next band.

When we came off the bandstand, I realized that everyone's face was tight.

"That was so messed up," Andréa murmured to me.

I could feel something in my body unclench. She was my best friend, and that director had pitted her against me. I hadn't realized how much I needed to know that she was on my side until I heard her words.

This camp promised to teach us about the music industry, but if they only wanted Taylor Swift types, then they should have said that.

As we sat, listening to the next band, I got a note on a napkin from Noelani.

Fatphobia much?

I felt the start of a smile on my face. Andréa leaned in and wrote,

Right? Fatphobic and racist?
Could this camp get any better?

Danielle grabbed the napkin and wrote,

Because of course all Black girls can rap. It was all I could do to keep from telling her our secret—we're in a gang! Let's rap about that gangsta life!

I stifled a laugh.

Casey looked over Danielle's shoulder and grabbed the pen.

No! Don't tell our secret. I'm a gangsta from the mean streets of Oahu. I still have cases open. THAT'S why they call me Casey!

This time, I couldn't totally hold it in. A guffaw managed to escape. But fortunately, the band had just finished, and everyone was clapping. The five of us cracked up for the twenty seconds that we had noise cancellation. Then we went back to sitting there, like this woman hadn't just shown a really ugly side of show business.

Then Casey leaned over to me. "I need my eyes," he said. "But I wish for a moment that I could give them to that woman. To everyone in the world who is literally narrow-minded. I wish they could see you the way I see you." I blushed. And for a moment, I felt . . . I don't know . . . sort of *avenged.* But then the insecurity came back. And the outrage.

◆ ◆ ◆

That night, I had trouble falling asleep. I was still mad at what the director had said. Yes, the band had talked a lot of mess about her, but it didn't erase her words. If this is how bad it felt to me, a spy, how awful would it be for a big girl who really *was* trying to make it in the music business? And it wasn't like she was telling me that the industry was fatphobic and I would need to fight hard. She was acting like *I* was the problem. Like something about *me* or *my* body needed to be fixed. Why wasn't she pointing to all the big, beautiful women who had made it in the music industry over the years?

I thought about Casey and how different it was to have someone fuss about my beauty from the first moment he saw me. I mean, yeah, it was also weird and way too much, and I didn't totally trust it. But more conventionally attractive girls were probably used to that type of attention all the time.

My mind was spinning. I couldn't seem to unwind for sleep. I slipped out the phone that Andréa had brought. If I had been home, I would have talked it out with my mom, but there was no way to do that here. Mom was always so clear. She had grown up in a community where women's bodies were accepted as beautiful in a really wide range of shapes and sizes. She always reinforced that these American attitudes were bigoted, fatphobic, and not based on anything other than prejudice, racism, and the need to keep women feeling bad about themselves.

I just needed some affirmation—someone to help me ground myself in that perspective. I went to MeVid and looked up "body acceptance." I got two ads for diets, but then I saw a picture of a Black spoken word artist who went by the name Supersizemic and clicked on one of her posts. It was a handheld video that one of her friends had shot, in a coffee shop. I put in earbuds and unmuted the sound.

Supersizemic was dark brown, with gold shadow on heavy-lidded eyes and a bold red lip. She wore a bright African print top and dark skirt. She looked out at the audience and grinned. "This poem is called 'Fat Girl on a Rampage.'"

The audience laughed and clapped, and a few women hooted.

"The date was blind & so were you
disappointed because I wasn't a size two
fool, I'm a woman not girl, shoot, I thought you knew
so this is for you & your whole sexist crew

If you want a scrawny girl, go out & get one
they're a dime a dozen 'cause they're sold by weight
wasting away on runways & burning themselves
  into nothing in gyms
but I am a woman of size with thighs and a shake
  to go with those fries
a prize despite media lies and the fact that men
  like you may not recognize

America loves these bread & water babes
eating like slaves
just enough to stay alive
slaving on diet plantations

picking at their food like cotton
& working out from can't see in the morning to
can't see at night
But I'm through with self-hate
I could be a size eight
but I've already got a job and I thought I had
a date
but I'll have to dismiss you if you want only
enough woman to survive
it could have been live
but you prefer a woman with a failure to thrive"

The video ended and I clicked the next one. It was called "Perfect." This one wasn't a live video. It was just her standing in front of a brick wall. Sort of confessional.

"the fashion model was a perfect size zero
which is perfect because
everybody loves a woman when she's
nothing

you are what you eat
so if you eat nothing
you, too, can be nothing

nothing from nothing leaves nothing
& if you eat nothing

you can feel nothing
think nothing
know nothing
remember nothing
say nothing
act like nothing ever happened

the fashion model was a perfect size zero
which is perfect because
everybody loves a woman when she's
nothing

to be or not to be
that IS the question"

Without the audience, it seemed a little anticlimactic. I began to search for another video of hers, but then I heard a noise in the cabin.

Quickly, I shut off the phone. I wasn't supposed to have it, and if Cassandra caught me, I'd get it confiscated. As a spy, I couldn't afford to lose my communication equipment, especially not for listening to spoken word. Although—given the day I'd had—it seemed like it was more than just entertainment. In that moment, hearing a fat Black girl talk about her own body with pride, hearing her shoot back at the fatphobia? It felt like survival.

FOURTEEN

The next day, we had our first songwriting class. They explained that everyone would take this class, whether they sang or not, and everyone would write a song. Later in the week, the teacher would meet one-on-one with each group's main songwriter.

Casey was our main songwriter, and if everyone was supposed to write a song, I wondered what I would write about. If I weren't a spy, it would definitely be something in the vein of Supersizemic. Sally wanted it to be personal, but I wasn't trying to write anything that personal.

Sally was giving us a songwriting pep talk.

"At this point, in the history of poetry, there's only one story that has never been told before: your story," she said, looking at all of us intensely. "Not the vague, general outlines but the specifics."

She flung out both arms. "Engage our senses," she said. "Show us the afternoon light on a lover's skin, as they walk away in the middle of a breakup. Describe the smell of a beloved family member's cooking that you haven't seen in years, or the sound of a siren arriving in the midst of a tragedy. Use the specifics! Reel us in! Music is about making people *feel* something. Use your words to make that happen."

She strode through the aisles between the desks in the classroom as she spoke.

"When something is really different but also manages to resonate deeply with audiences, that can break through the noise. And that's what we're here to see if we can find."

Her gaze roved across the class.

"Most of your bands have a lead songwriter," she went on. "But we have *everyone* write a song here. We find that there are often hidden gems written by the musicians who don't usually write. Our job is to get you out of your comfort zone. For the usual songwriters, try writing about something new. And for everyone, tell the story that is *your* story, burning inside you, waiting to be told. That is what I'm looking for from you in this workshop. So get your pens and papers out now and *go*!"

I felt a heaviness in my gut, and Andréa and I exchanged a glance. The story burning inside Danielle to be told? That was bad. I could see her already scribbling furiously. Maybe this creativity outlet for her was a terrible idea.

But there was nothing I could do for the next twenty minutes. Instead, I tried to think of a song idea that wouldn't blow my cover but was something I could stand to work on for the next week.

I decided to write a girl power anthem. I wouldn't clap back to the fatphobia specifically, but I would clap back in general.

When you fight so hard to be bold
But they try to crush the dreams you hold
And when the broken pieces fall
You want to disappear back against the wall
But now is not the time to go small

Yes! I didn't need to talk specifically about fatphobia, but it could be a double-meaning metaphor.

Play it big! Don't let your fear make
the choice for you.
Play it big! What were you put here
on earth to do?
Play it big! What are you scared that
someone will say?
What matters most at the end of the day?
Did you come here to watch or come here
to play? Well, I came to play it big.

“Nice work,” Sally said. “I saw a lot of pens moving fast.”

What? Was that twenty minutes already?

I peeked over at Danielle. She looked intense—sort of like she might cry but also sort of triumphant. I cut a look at Andréa in the other direction. Apparently, she had seen it, too.

This was definitely not good.

But there was no time to sneak away for a strategy conversation with Andréa or to initiate a heart-to-heart with Danielle. Because today the whole camp had a special lunch with some woman who was a music producer.

I leaned over to Danielle anyway. “You had a really intense expression on your face in songwriting class,” I said. “Is everything okay?”

Before she could respond, the head counselor shushed me. “Show our guest some respect,” she hissed.

The producer was very LA. Thin as a skeleton, big blond hair, and a fake-looking tan. She kept talking about that “hotty-hotness factor.” It seemed to come down to the same thing everyone else was saying: the market wanted the same old thing, but with some kind of minor modification to keep it from being stale.

Not only was her talk kind of offensive, but it was also boring. After a while, I began to tune out and write the second verse of my song in my head:

Teeny tiny Barbie chicks
That the media depicts
Want to keep us all contained
But with me, they'll try in vain
Sit back and let me explain
Play it big! Don't let your fear make the choice for you.
Play it big! What were you put here on earth to do?
Play it big! What are you scared that someone will say?
What matters most at the end of the day?
Did you come here to watch or come here to play?
Well, I came to play it big.

A moment later, Andréa nudged me hard. She tilted her head subtly toward the left. I looked where she indicated and saw Danielle bent over her notebook, jaw clenched. She was scribbling hard, like, almost tearing the paper.

Uh-oh!

I wrote on the corner of my notebook. Andréa underlined it and added an exclamation point.

I tried to talk to Danielle all evening, but she offered nothing but monosyllabic responses. Usually, when it came to parent-child conflicts, I sympathized with the kid. But after an evening of trying to get Danielle to talk to me, I started to sympathize with her mom, Sheila.

We brushed our teeth and got ready for lights-out. An hour later, I was still awake on the bottom bunk when I felt the bed creaking—Danielle was getting out of bed! I opened my eyes just a slit. The cabin was illuminated by moonlight, and I could see Danielle climbing down the ladder fully dressed. She grabbed her sneakers by the door and opened it carefully. After she closed it, I slipped out of bed, shaking Andréa awake on my way.

Andréa popped up and our eyes met.

Below her bunk, I was surprised to see that Noelani's bed was empty. How had she gotten out so quietly? But I guess I had been listening for Danielle and not her.

Andréa and I opened the door carefully and saw Danielle heading across the clearing. Andréa and I grabbed our shoes and jackets and slipped out to follow her.

The two of us hopped across the grass, pulling on sneakers as we watched Danielle disappear into the woods. Fortunately, there was a wide trail, and I hoped she would be following it. We hustled to catch up.

We crossed the grass at a half run. But when we hit the trail, the terrain got rockier and our footsteps made more noise on the hard dirt. Which was good—as far as being able to hear Danielle and follow her—but not great for us to travel with any stealth. The two of us walked as silently as we could, following Danielle's footsteps ahead.

Abruptly, she stopped making noise, and Andréa and I locked eyes in the moonlight. I waved to her to go ahead. She nodded. I hoped she understood what I was trying to say. When I heard her walking noisily along the trail, I knew she got the plan: she would keep going while I waited just in case Danielle had slipped out of sight off the path and was hiding.

Crunch! Crunch! Crunch! went Andréa's loud footsteps.

I waited about a minute and, sure enough, footsteps began again. I rushed around a curve and saw a shadowy figure ahead on the path.

I called her name: "Danielle!"

She startled and turned around.

"Oh my God, you almost gave me a heart attack!" she gasped.

"Where are you going?" I asked.

I heard running footsteps ahead of us.

"Hide if you don't want to get busted!" Danielle hissed.

"It's just Andréa," I said as she came into view ahead of us on the trail. "And you didn't answer my question."

"I'm going on a nature walk?" Danielle said.

"Bullshit," I said as we caught up to Andréa.

"Okay, fine," Danielle said. "I'm meeting Noelani and Casey."

"For what?" I asked.

"Promise you won't tell?" she asked.

"What," I said, "and get you all kicked out so I lose my shot at winning?"

"Yeah," Andréa said. "We're in this together."

Danielle rolled her eyes and pulled something out from under her jacket. It was a flat bottle of liquor. Wait, two. No, three!

"Oh my God," I said, forcing a grin. "Where did you get all that?"

I glanced up at Andréa. Her face was shocked and a little horrified, but I gave her a sort of urgent-grin face, and she caught on.

"Yeah," Andréa said. "Score! Let's go."

"I thought you guys would be more judgy," Danielle said.

"No way," I said. "We like to kick it just as much as anyone."

"Yeah," Andréa said. She was smiling, but even in the moonlight, I could see tense lines on her face.

FIFTEEN

We walked in silence for a few more minutes before we got to a fork in the road. Danielle howled like a coyote, and someone howled back.

"Was that Casey or Noelani?" Andréa asked.

"Casey," Danielle said. "Noelani's howl sounds ridiculous. She does a good birdcall, though."

The three of us cut to the right, in the direction of the howl, onto a much narrower trail. It was really dark under the trees, and Danielle pulled out her flashlight to guide the way. She howled again and got a return howl. Then we veered farther off the trail, and suddenly we were in a circle of stumps, with our other two band members.

"You brought company?" Noelani asked.

"A welcome surprise," Casey said, grinning.

"Okay," Andréa said. "How were you all going to sneak out and have a party without us?"

"We didn't want you to get in trouble," Danielle said.

"We didn't know if you liked to drink," Casey said, looking straight at me.

"Basically," Noelani said, "we didn't know if you would rat us out."

"Like we told Danielle," I said, "if you get in trouble, it kills our chances of winning, too."

"Nobody wants that," Andréa said.

"Glad we got that settled," Casey said, coming over to put an arm around me.

I felt butterflies in my stomach, but I ducked out from under his arm.

"So what are we drinking?" I asked, sidling up to Danielle.

I tried to sound like I was experienced in these things, but basically I had tried alcohol on only one previous occasion. I had been at a winter dance where a friend had a bottle, and I'd had some. Apparently, that had been gin. I couldn't tell you the difference between one type of alcohol and another.

According to Danielle, we were drinking rum. Casey had little paper cups from the bathroom. I knew from my Caribbean history that rum was made from sugarcane, but it didn't taste sweet like a soda. It burned when it went down. Not that I took a big drink—just a little bit. I saw that Andréa took an even smaller sip than me—maybe nothing at all. And then she tipped the cup into the grass when no one was looking. Smart move. I did the same.

Danielle did the opposite. She filled the little cup and drank it quickly, throwing her head back. Then she refilled it and did it again twice. Her whole energy changed after that. It wasn't possible that the alcohol was already impacting her with full force. I happened to know that it took fifteen minutes at the very least to get the total effect. But she sat back, eager already, waiting for the feeling to hit her.

Casey took two shots. Noelani sipped, like Andréa and I did. But she didn't tip hers into the grass.

Half an hour later, Danielle and Casey were laughing and singing loudly.

"Shhhh!" Noelani shushed them. "Who's trying to get us busted now?"

"We're far enough away from the camp," Danielle slurred. "They'll never hear us . . ." She began to sing our song. Her voice was strong and her tone lovely.

"Danielle," I said, "how come you don't sing lead?"

"Because," she said, "I don't have this liquid courage when I go onstage." She took another swig of the alcohol.

"I've been telling her for ages that she should sing," Noelani said.

"We all have," Casey said. "But instead, I was stuck

singing lead. I'm the man behind the scenes! We need someone bee-you-tee-ful to be our lead singer. Thass why I'm so glad you came, Imani. You've got it all. The voice. The beee-you-tee. You're a ten. No! No! You're an LA ten and a Portland eleven."

He and Noelani high-fived. What? Why was she encouraging him to rate girls—rate *me*? I mean, it was nice to be considered both a ten and more than ten. But if it could be higher than ten, then did the numbers even mean anything?

Andréa gave me a quizzical look. I hadn't told her about Casey's crush or whatever it was. Or about whatever I was feeling. I'd thought it had cooled off. But I guessed the booze brought out Danielle's singing and Casey's flirting.

"Hey!" came a voice. "Is someone out there?"

We all froze. It sounded like one of the male counselors. Fortunately, we were sitting behind a rock, and there was enough moon that we didn't have any lanterns on. No one could see us from the trail.

Soon, we could see a flashlight beam bobbing along. It swung in a wide arc and pointed our way, but it wasn't strong enough to reach us. We stayed quiet, not giving the counselor a reason to come in our direction.

When he had headed far enough past us on the trail, Andréa hissed that we should head back.

"Definitely," Noelani said, standing up.

I stood, too.

"Let's not go back yet," Casey said, taking my hand. He tried to pull me back down. His grip was heavy and awkward.

"No, seriously," Noelani said. "We need to get back to camp before he does. If he sounds the alarm, they'll do a bed check, and if they find we're not there, they'll kick us out of camp."

"They won't catch us," Danielle declared. "I'm gonna be opera mystic."

"You're what?" Noelani asked.

"Option mythic," Danielle tried again.

"Optimistic?" Andréa asked.

"That one," Danielle agreed.

"Remember," Noelani said, "you don't want to spend the rest of the summer cooped up all day with your mom."

"I really do not," Danielle agreed. Then she began to cry. "It's too sad with just the two of us in that tiny space. Too, too sad. You just don't know . . ."

I didn't want her to finish that sentence. At least not with the others listening. "And we're gonna make sure you don't have to go to that sad place," I said. "Let's get back to our cabin. Let's make sure."

I knelt down next to her, and Andréa knelt down on her other side. We put her arms over our shoulders and pulled her up to her feet.

"I'm so lucky to have friends like you looking out for me," she said. "So lucky."

Andréa and I were walking her carefully toward the path.

"Lucky, lucky, lucky," she said.

"Shhh!" Andréa shushed her. "We don't want them to hear us."

Danielle nodded solemnly and put a finger to her lips.

I looked behind us. Noelani was walking pretty well and sort of helping Casey along. Then she sent him on his way toward the boys' side.

Meanwhile, we girls made our way back to camp without incident. The challenge was going to be sneaking back into bed in the cabin.

"What's our plan?" Andréa asked.

"I'm not sure," I said. "We've got to get her up to that top bunk."

Andréa nodded. "Can we lift her up?"

"I don't think so," I said. "But maybe we can give her a boost."

She nodded again.

"Okay, I have an idea," I said. "It would make sense for Danielle to get up to pee. Maybe we send her to the bathroom."

"That's good!" Andréa said. "It'll work if the rest of us are in bed."

"Okay," I said. "Let me do some recon." I tiptoed into the cabin and stood near our counselor. She seemed to be breathing evenly and slowly. Good.

"Cassandra is sound asleep," I whispered to our little crew when I got back outside. "So here's the plan. Andréa and I can go in and lie down in our bunks. Noelani, are you good to get to your bunk quietly?"

She nodded.

"Good," I said. "You walk Danielle to the bathroom. Danielle, your job is just to flush the toilet, then walk back to bed. I'll pretend that the flush woke me up and I'll get up. I'll boost you up to your bunk, then go to the bathroom myself."

"Good," Danielle said. "Because I really do need to pee."

"Let's all get our shoes and jackets off before we go in," Andréa said. "We need to set them down quietly on the way in."

"Yes. Excellent. Is everyone clear on the plan?" I asked.

Everyone nodded. Danielle looked iffy, but we were gonna help her.

"Okay," Andréa said. "Let's do this."

Andréa and I went first, carefully dropping all our shoes and hanging up our jackets. Meanwhile, Noelani walked Danielle to the bathroom, then tiptoed to her lower bunk.

She had barely gotten in when I heard the toilet flush.

Cassandra stirred in her bed.

I sat up and rubbed my eyes like I was just waking up. But it took a while for Danielle to come back from the bathroom, and she was wobbly when she came out. Luckily Cassandra rolled over and went back to sleep.

When Danielle made it to our bunk bed, I stood up. She swayed a bit, and I placed her hands on the ladder rungs. This was a two-person job. Fortunately, Andréa saw that I was struggling and came over to help. Between the two of us, we boosted Danielle up, and I rolled her into bed. Thank goodness the bed was against the wall; otherwise, she might have fallen out the other side.

Obviously, Danielle's drinking was a problem—not only for her (not the healthiest way to deal with her issues!) but also for the Factory. I wanted to talk to Andréa about it, but there was no time. Our cover within a cover was that we had been sleeping.

I lay in bed and took deep breaths until it was true.

SIXTEEN

At breakfast, both Danielle and Casey looked like crap. But Noelani looked the same as always. I hoped that I did, too.

"I'm super excited about our songwriting workshop today," Noelani said. "I'm gonna write a song for Sarita and send it to her."

"Why are you so damn cheerful?" Danielle asked with a sour expression.

"It's a beautiful day," Noelani said.

"I beg to differ," Casey said.

"You all need to drink more water," Noelani said. "When you drink, be aware and practice self-care."

Andréa missed breakfast, but I caught up to her on the way to songwriting class. "Are you okay?" I asked.

Her face shifted abruptly to a smile. "Yeah," she said, "I'm fine. Just tired."

But something seemed off.

"Andréa," I said, "it's me. What's going on?"

She looked at me, then looked around. "I feel sort of unprofessional," she said. "I should be able to handle it."

"Come on," I said. "You gotta let your team know what's going on. And I'm your team."

"I guess—" she began. "I just sort of got . . . I mean, the drinking. It just . . ." She blew out her breath. "My dad's family has a lot of alcoholism. His dad—my grandfather—was an alcoholic, so my papi doesn't drink at all. He explained to us that among Indigenous folks, alcohol was part of the campaign of genocide. That it's still a problem for lots of Indigenous communities today. I guess— I've never even tried it before. I was scared it would— I would, I don't know. Really want more, or something."

"How did you feel when you drank last night?" I asked.

"I'm not sure," she said. "I didn't actually drink it."

"Wow," I said. "Good job. It looked so real."

"Yeah," she said. "I was proud that I figured out how not to blow my cover, but also how not to drink." She huffed out a breath. "It's good to get that off my chest. Thank you."

"Anytime," I said.

• • •

In songwriting class that day, Danielle was downright surly.

"How can I possibly be cursed with this level of headache at a music camp with loud instruments?" she asked. "Shoot me now."

Noelani shook her head. "Next time we partake, I'll bring extra water and share my aspirin."

To make things worse, the teacher had this nature metaphor going. "What is the weather for your song?" she asked, strolling between the desks. "Are you a sunny day? A rainbow over the ocean? A passionate tempest? A hurricane of destruction?"

It was clear that Danielle was the last one. And the mention of hurricanes can't have helped much, either.

But there was nothing I could do. Danielle was plugged in to a keyboard, headphones on. She was mutter-humming a tune and scribbling hard in her notebook.

I tried to keep working on my girl power anthem, but Danielle's erratic movements kept catching my attention out of the corner of my eye. I swiveled my body some, and on the other side of me, Andréa was also scribbling furiously.

In the back, Casey was slumped over his notebook in a stupor, his pen seeming to be doodling in circles. Only Noelani was calm, looking off into space for a bit, then writing at a leisurely pace and smiling occasionally. Apparently, her love song for Sarita was going well, and it wasn't a tempest but a rainbow over the ocean.

Danielle stayed grumpy all day, so I was surprised when, over dinner, she said that she wanted to sneak out again that night. Andréa and I shared glances, but I couldn't think of a way to stop her—if we said we didn't want to go, she would just go ahead without us. At least if we came along, we could do damage control.

When we got to what we were now calling "the rock," Casey had already started drinking without us. He was even more drunk than the night before. And what did he have in his hands? As I came closer, I realized it was a ukulele.

"Imani," he said. "Beautiful Imani, come sit by me."

He was sort of adorable. But also sort of obnoxious.

I smiled. "I'm gonna stay standing," I said. "But thanks for the offer."

Andréa had had the great idea to bring along a bottle filled with tea so that we could drink that and pretend it was alcohol instead of having to drink the rum.

On the one hand, her plan worked great, but on the other hand, that meant there was more for everyone else. Danielle did four shots this time, and Noelani did two. An hour later, everyone was pretty drunk except me and Andréa, but we managed to act pretty drunk.

"I wrote you a song," Casey said to me. I guess he

thought he was whispering in my ear, but everyone could hear.

Danielle laughed out loud. Andréa gave me a look.

He strummed a few chords on the ukulele.

"I-ma-niiii," he sang. *"She put a love spell on me!"*

I couldn't quite move. I just thanked goodness for the dark that kept my face in shadow.

"Her beauty takes my breath away, a single smile from her can make my day . . ."

I looked away from Casey and stared off into space. Danielle kept laughing.

"And her voice—" Casey went on, but then he hit a wrong chord. *"Her voice—"* he tried again but couldn't seem to get the chord right.

"You guys, I really miss Sarita," Noelani said. "I hate that I don't have my phone to call her."

"She knows you love her," Danielle said. "She'll understand."

"But it's not just that," Noelani said. "I want to know how her trip to India is going. It's her first trip to the homeland. Such a big deal, and I'm missing it."

As I listened to Noelani, I noticed that when she talked about Sarita, she was really curious about how Sarita was doing. How did her girlfriend feel? What was she experiencing? She wanted to talk to her. She wanted to *listen* to her. I noticed that Casey mostly talked about how I made *him* feel. He didn't ever really ask me anything about myself . . .

"You're right, Noelani," Andréa said. "It's a big deal to visit your homeland. I've visited both of my homelands: Puerto Rico and Mexico. They were both a big deal, but Mexico was a bigger deal because it's . . . well . . . much bigger." She laughed at her own joke.

"I just don't know what that's like," Noelani said. "I'm Native Hawaiian. I've always been in my homeland."

"As an African American," Casey piped up, "I've never been in my homeland."

"I'm Caribbean American," Danielle said. "I've never been to my homeland, either. My mom is from Barbados."

"I didn't know that," I said. But of course, I totally did.

"It's the birthplace of rum," she said, and took another swig from her bottle. "And it features prominently in my new song. Wanna hear it?"

"Yes, please!" Noelani said. "I love your songs. You haven't written a new one in so long."

"It's better with the keyboard," Danielle said. "But here goes."

Danielle pulled a piece of paper from her pocket. It was a page from her notebook, apparently the one with the lyrics to her new song. The tune was super catchy, and at first I nodded along.

"Rum is made of sugar
Pressed from sugarcane

I drink it to forget you
The one from whom I came
Crystals bright and sparkling
Whitewashing all the truth
That day I found the papers
And got down to the root

You sugarcoated it
The truth about our lives
You sugarcoated it
The way my father died
You sugarcoated it
The fact he was a spy

When I learned we lived a lie"

I felt a spike of fear when I heard the word "spy," but I tried to keep my expression neutral.

"I thought I had an uncle
Family extended to a guy
Who seemed like Dad's closest friend
He was always coming by
Turned out he wasn't family
Extended or otherwise
My father's spying colleague
Uncle Dayvon was a lie"

She was naming her father's partner? No! This couldn't get any worse.

"I know they both were agents
I finally broke the code
I learned that Dad was shot down
On that Charleston road
But lying was the pistol
Lying was the knife
Lying was the atom bomb
That blew up our life"

I was wrong. This was *definitely* worse. She named the city where her dad had died. And then she sang the chorus again:

"You sugarcoated it
The truth about our lives"

Andréa and I were staring at each other in horror. Not only was Danielle saying outright that her father was a spy, but she was also laying out a trail of flares that led right to the Factory and to our agent in the field. Any enemies of our work who could do a little digging would be able to connect all the dots. This was a disaster.

"Wow!" Noelani said. "That was amazing. Let's record it!"

"Yeah," Casey said. "That needs to be our next song that we work on. It was hard-core."

"I don't know, guys," Andréa said. "It's pretty late. We should, like, head back. We can do it later."

"No way," Casey said. "You gotta document the deep creative moments. Record her first and me next."

"Definitely," Noelani said. She was pulling out her digital recorder.

So Andréa and I watched as Danielle basically spilled the secrets that we were sworn to protect.

"he was a spy

. . .

spying colleague Uncle Dayvon

. . .

shot down on that Charleston road"

The worst part of watching her record the song was remembering to fix my face to look encouraging—not like every line was itself a weapon to destroy my world.

SEVENTEEN

When Danielle was done, we applauded, the clapping sounding hollow among the sounds of the night.

"Well," Andréa said, "now that our private concert's over, do we wanna head back?"

Everyone agreed. Danielle and Casey were pretty smashed. I helped Danielle up, and Andréa and Noelani helped Casey.

Halfway back to the cabins, Casey piped up.

"Hey," he said, "I never got to finish my song."

"Next time," Andréa promised.

Ugh. That guy was gonna keep trying. And then it hit me. I needed to keep trying, too. Okay, so Noelani had recorded Danielle's song. But she was drunk. Everyone was drunk except for Andréa and me. What if we could get the recorder? What if we could destroy it? Could we walk by the pond on the way back? Accidentally drop it in?

But Danielle would still have the lyrics. Or would she? Hadn't she put them in her pocket? She was drunk. It ought to be easy enough to pickpocket her.

My arm was already around her waist. I just had to lean a little farther and slip the paper out. Nobody noticed. Even she didn't notice.

Wow. Note to self: Don't get drunk and carry anything in your pockets that you really need. It was just too easy for someone to take it without you knowing.

I tried to sidle up next to Noelani. Which pocket had she put the recorder in? I sort of leaned on her and reached toward the pocket of her hoodie.

"Hello, friend!" she said, and put an arm around me. She gave a squeeze, but then she let go.

She wasn't quite as drunk as Danielle. She was fully aware of her body. No way I was getting that recorder.

"Imani?"

I realized someone was saying my name. "Huh?"

It was Casey. Andréa was helping him, but he started weaving sort of side to side as he leaned on her. Noelani went over to help.

"Don't *you* want to hear the rest of my song?" Casey asked me.

"I think it's amazing that you wrote the song so quickly," I said. "And it's really flattering. But it's also sort of awkward."

"Awkward?" he asked. "My song is awkward? How can my declarations of love be awkward? Dang. How come the beautiful ones never like me back?" He looked up at the sky. "Why?!"

Noelani jumped in.

"Case, we talked about this last time," she said. "When you have a crush on someone, you come on too strong, and it sort of drives them away. You need to learn to turn down the volume. Get to know the person. Figure out what they like. Not everyone likes to be swept up in an avalanche of intense romantic gestures."

Wasn't that the truth?

But if he appreciated the good advice, Casey didn't thank her. In fact, he didn't say another word. He just sort of sulked the whole way back.

On the bright side, however, I wouldn't need to tell Andréa about the crush. It was all out there now.

And watching Casey stagger down the trail, something settled in me; it was the word "no." No, I didn't like him like that. It had been flattering to have him come on so strong. We had had a couple of . . . moments . . . but it didn't feel right. There was such a contrast between how he talked about me and how Noelani talked about Sarita. And the thing she'd said to him: "Get to know the person." It was as if Casey liked . . . the *image* of me. Or the idea of me. But he kind of hadn't bothered to get to know me at all.

This was a spy operation, and I needed to stay

focused. But beyond that, I didn't even *want* to get to know him in that way. So what if he thought I was beautiful? That didn't mean I owed him anything. I needed to just focus on the singing and the mission.

As we approached the cabins, Casey walked toward the boys' side, and we veered to the girls' side. We all whispered good night to him, but he just walked in the direction of his cabin without a word.

"Is he gonna be okay getting back in?" I asked.

Noelani rolled her eyes in the moonlight. "They monitor the girls much more closely than the boys. He'll be fine."

Apparently, they weren't monitoring us too closely, either. Because we pulled the return-to-bed trick a second time, and it worked like a charm.

So fifteen minutes later, I was lying in bed trying to figure out what to do. Our mission had basically failed, right? It seemed like it was too dangerous to keep Danielle here now. What if she sang that song in public? What if we *won*? With all the eyes on that song, it wouldn't take much for someone to become suspicious. The safest thing to do was to send Danielle and her mom away, like Jerrold had planned. But my heart ached for her, being torn away from her home and her friends. Would she ever get the help she needed?

I felt a tug on my ankle and saw Andréa motioning me to get up.

I slid from the bed quietly and followed her out the cabin door.

"Well, our mission is over," I said on the cabin porch. "After that song, it's basically a failure."

"Or is it?" Andréa asked, producing Noelani's digital recorder from her pocket.

"Oh wow!" I said. "I tried to get it out of her pocket."

"I had already swiped it back at the rock," Andréa said.

"So do we delete it?"

"We could," she said. "But I think I have a better idea."

"Erase their memories?"

"Actually, sort of," Andréa said. "What if we send it to the Factory and have them change it up? Make it different, garbled?"

"That's brilliant!" I said.

Andréa grinned at me. "Now the only problem is that Danielle still has the hard copy of the lyrics."

"Or does she?" I asked, pulling the paper out of my pajama top pocket.

Andréa grinned and clapped her hands silently. "¡Carajo!" she said, grinning. "Best team ever."

I hooked up the recorder to my phone and sent the file to our tech team at the Factory. They said to go to sleep and that they would get it done.

Just before sunrise, Andréa woke me up, and we

snuck back outside. The Factory had sent back an audio file.

Rum is made of sugar
Pressed from sugarcane
I drink it to forget you
The one from whom I came
Crystals bright and sparkling
Whitewashing all the pain
Our family was all sunshine
Now it's only rain

You sugarcoated it
The pain inside our lives
You sugarcoated it
You just work and never cry
You sugarcoated it
The outside looks so nice
Like bitter-centered candy
I swallow every night

I know your pain is ancient
I knew it from the start
The lesson of the islands
Is never fall apart
But if you fake forever
Then I must be the one

To show the bitter truth
While everyone looks on

And then she sang the chorus again:

You sugarcoated it
The pain inside our lives
You sugarcoated it
You just work and never cry
You sugarcoated it
The outside looks so nice
Like bitter-centered candy
I swallow every night

By the end, our mouths were falling open.

"That was amazing!" Andréa said. "It sounds just like her."

"And the lyrics manage to include the angst but make no mention of the Factory stuff," I said. "It's just about how her mom was such a robot since her dad died."

"Still," Andréa said, "I'm afraid it won't be enough to stop her from blowing her cover eventually."

"Let's just deal with one threat at a time," I said. "We need to take the W on this one and be ready for the next one."

EIGHTEEN

By the time we were done, the sun was up, and campers were definitely moving around.

I started running. "Let's say we went for a jog," I said to Andréa.

"Good idea," she said, and began to jog alongside me.

When we got back to the cabin, Danielle was still in bed. But Cassandra was awake.

"Where'd you two go?" she asked.

"Out for a run," I said. "Just a short one."

"I didn't know you girls liked to run," Cassandra said. "I might go with you tomorrow."

Uh-oh. I hadn't counted on that.

"I don't go every day," Andréa said. "I like to run every other day and alternate with weight-bearing exercises. I do lifts with my guitar."

I just nodded along, glad that she had such a good answer.

"I can't find my digital recorder anywhere," Noelani said.

"You had it yesterday at . . . uh . . . dinner," I said.

"Did you look by the door?" Andréa asked.

"Yeah," Noelani said.

"Did you look behind the shoe rack under the coat hooks?" Andréa asked, walking over to the door. "Something of mine fell behind there yesterday and—"

She leaned down and "found" the recorder.

"Yes!" Noelani said with a grin, and hugged her. "I have the melody for Sarita's song on there. And Danielle's song."

Not really. She had the fake version of Danielle's song after we had carefully deleted and replaced Danielle's song on the recorder. But I didn't tell her that.

Danielle came back to life more easily than she had the day before, and it was nice to spend some time with her in a better mood. There had been no sign of Casey, but the rest of us were sitting around after breakfast.

"That water-and-aspirin trick was a lifesaver," Danielle said to Noelani.

"Let's listen to your song," Noelani suggested.

Andréa and I looked at each other as Noelani took the recorder out of her pocket.

You sugarcoated it
The pain inside our lives
You sugarcoated it
You just work and never cry . . .

"That's so weird," Danielle said. "It's not as good as I remember. It's sort of . . . missing something."

"Really?" I asked. "It's exactly how I remember it from last night."

"Yeah," Andréa agreed. Then she began to sing. "'*You sugarcoated it. The pain inside our lives.*' It's been running in my head all night. It's catchy."

Noelani laughed. "Hoo, girl," she said. "That's why I don't drink all the time—because alcohol distorts your perceptions."

I almost felt bad, gaslighting them like that. But it was for a good cause. And alcohol can distort perceptions. That was just . . . not what actually happened this particular time.

But my relief was short-lived. That day in songwriting class, Danielle was hyper intense while writing. Again.

Toward the end of class, the teacher invited us to share some of our lyrics.

"Before I open the floor today," Sally said, "I want to remind everyone that this is a confidential space. I am asking you all to dig deep into what's personal and intimate to you. So what we share in here stays in here. Does everyone agree to that?"

There was a murmur of assent.

"Oh, no," she said. "We need actual consent language. I want everyone who agrees to say, 'Yes!' "

She strode out from behind her desk. "Does everyone agree to keep what they hear in the songs confidential?"

"Yes!" we chorused back.

"All right," she said. "Who would like to begin?"

A guy in a black leather jacket raised his hand. Dude. Who wears leather in this heat? He had dyed black hair, and the rest of his clothes were black as well.

His song was all about loneliness, extended metaphors of barren landscapes and postwar battlefields. It was definitely a downer.

After he was done, Danielle tentatively raised her hand. I hoped she was going to sing the doctored version of her song, but she had written something new. Something even worse.

"My mother dealt in secrets
My mother was a spy
That lifestyle killed my father
Then it was only she and I

You minded everyone's business but your own
You were blinded by your profession

And you left me all alone

You said it was for freedom
For our people, proud and Black
But when it took my father
You falsified the facts

You minded everyone's business but your own
You were blinded by your profession
And you left me all alone

He died in the line of duty
When a bullet struck
You said it was a car crash
Your lie destroyed my trust

After years of silence
I finally broke the code
I learned that he was shot down
On that Charleston road"

Ugh! That dang "code/road" rhyme was back? Clearly, erasing the recording did nothing to erase her memory. This was really bad.

"I thought I knew my father
I thought I could relax

And trust in what he told me
But now I know the facts
He was a secret agent
For some Black operation
Some rogue organization
Not loyal to any nation"

I tried to take a deep breath, and it caught a bit in my throat. I hoped no one noticed. I couldn't look at Andréa.

"You minded everyone's business but your own
You were blinded by your profession
And you left me all alone"

When the song was over, I sat there, stunned. All our work from last night was for nothing? We had changed the lyrics only for her to write a new version that was even more lethal? "Black operation"? "Rogue organization"? The only thing missing in this version was naming her father's partner.

But then, as if it wasn't bad enough, Danielle began to say *more.*

"My mother . . . worked in the intelligence field. And . . . well, I guess the rest is in the song." Danielle looked like she was on the verge of tears. "I know it might sound like I made it up, but it's all true."

"Excellent work, Danielle," Sally said. "I'm very

proud of you. I think you really found the words to tell your story."

I had to agree. And the thought had me completely panicked. I still couldn't look at Andréa. The situation felt so urgent. My only shred of hope was the fact that we had all been sworn to confidentiality. Maybe this was just Danielle doing a sort of journal entry. Maybe it was too personal for her to try to sing for the contest. I mentally crossed my fingers that would be the case.

A few more students shared. Their stuff was much more predictable romance stuff: unrequited love, breakups.

"Good work, everyone," Sally said as the class was ending. "Now, I am expecting everyone to adhere to our confidentiality agreement. As artists, you will often be expected to sign nondisclosure agreements. Huge amounts of money might be at stake if you break those NDAs. This is your first professional test."

Confidentiality or no confidentiality, I needed to get on the phone with Jerrold right away.

NINETEEN

But before I had a chance to check in with the Factory, we had some even worse news. At dinner, the director told us that there were two wildfires in the area. They weren't very close to us, but they were between us and the highway.

There was a murmur throughout the camp as we processed this news.

"There's no need to panic," said the director. "Fortunately, the wind is sending the fires in the other direction, not toward us. And the smoke is mostly heading away, too."

That was lucky. I had caught the scent of smoke outside before dinner, and I was glad that it wasn't worse.

"While some of the towns in the area have issued

advisories to stay indoors, our air quality is still moderate. Make sure you drink extra water, and please stay close to camp—no long hikes. We'll be monitoring the situation, and we want you to be close by in case there's a sudden change and we need to evacuate."

We all exchanged nervous glances.

Danielle murmured, "At least they're not sending us home," and Noelani gave her a nod.

The director went on. "The roads are too dangerous to travel, so we'll be cut off for a couple of days. That means no fresh produce, but don't worry—the camp is well supplied with canned veggies and frozen foods."

But I couldn't think about the food supply chain. This was a disaster for our operation. It felt like Danielle was on the brink of spilling everything, and now there was no way to get her out of there. I looked at Andréa in alarm, but we couldn't discuss the situation in front of everyone.

Casey came in late to dinner.

"Dude," Noelani asked. "Where have you been? You missed an announcement about wildfires."

"Writing!" he said triumphantly, totally ignoring the idea of fires. "I have an amazing new song. And I want to put it in the ring for the contest. I think it's the one."

"You're not the only one who's been writing great stuff, you know," Noelani said. "Danielle wrote an amazing song today. The teacher loved it."

"Enough said," Andréa piped up. "Confidentiality."

Noelani zipped her lips. "Just saying," she told Casey. "You might have some competition at band meeting tomorrow."

"Bring it on," Casey said, grinning. He went to go get a tray of tuna casserole and continued to smile throughout dinner as he ate it. The casserole was awful, so he must have been in a really good mood.

All throughout the meal, he was super friendly in my direction. I smiled and replied, but the chemistry between us was gone. At least on my end.

After dinner, I made an excuse and found a quiet spot to call Jerrold. I caught him up on everything that was happening.

"That's not good. Is there any way to get Danielle out of there?" he asked.

"They said that the roads are restricted to emergency vehicles only, until they get the fire contained. I think we'll have to sit tight until then."

"We could send a helicopter, but it would be a little hard to keep that under the radar," Jerrold said. "I think that our only option is to wait this out. Can you stick close to Danielle? Try your best to keep her from giving everything away?"

"Yes."

"There's one more issue that you might not be aware of," he said. "Have you heard that Monty Hughes of Zemazin is the new sponsor of the competition?"

This was news to me. Zemazin was a massive online shopping corporation that had its trucks delivering every type of thing all over the world. My family didn't buy from them, because they apparently treated their workers so badly that they didn't even get breaks to go to the bathroom.

Jerrold went on: "Imani, Zemazin is the company where we have our biggest current operation. We need to be extra careful. I'm putting together an extraction team that will be on standby for when the road opens up. Meanwhile, I want morning and evening reports from you."

"Absolutely," I said.

TWENTY

I lay in bed later that night, waiting for Cassandra to fall asleep so we could sneak out. But instead of pretending to sleep, I texted Andréa an update. I also looked up Monty Hughes. Apparently, he was based out of Silicon Valley, California—the nation's tech capital. At first, I just found lots of photos of him smiling in front of his various cars, boats, houses, and offices. But after I dug beneath the magazine puff pieces and fawning profiles, I found some shadowy stuff.

First of all, he had been a climate denier. He had insisted that climate change was a total hoax until 2010. Since then, his team had backpedaled, insisting he had just been "a bit skeptical" and "waiting until the scientists weren't in so much disagreement." But an angry climate activist had posted a blog entry called "Monty Hughes: Climate Denial Receipts." In it, she posted a ton of quotes with links, where he said stuff like "I don't care what scientists say; I like hot weather." And "I won't stop driving my gas-guzzling car till the day I die."

That blog post also linked a number of organizations that his charity funded. They included things like "Beautification Projects" that undertook the restoration of Confederate statues and "Alternative Teen Girls' Empowerment" that included a "level-up" course on how to go from having a boyfriend to having a fiancé. A deep dive into their curriculum found lessons like "How to guarantee a senior-year marriage proposal" and "Hitched by the end of high school."

So this guy liked to beautify the legacy of slavery and get teenage girls married off before—or maybe instead of—going to college? Gross. I took some screenshots and sent them to Andréa, along with some links.

And I added a GIF of a unicorn throwing up for good measure.

Andréa replied with a GIF of a vomiting Pokémon and some other links to Monty Hughes's history. Apparently, he had a bunch of affiliations that he never came right out and claimed officially. For example, during the era of the right-wing group the Tea Party, he never officially said he supported them, but he was always posing drinking tea and winking. And later, after the January 6, 2021, storming of the Capitol, he adopted a white kitten whom he named "Stormer" and had the cat in every social media post for the next couple of months.

"This guy is such a creep!" I texted to Andréa.

"Tell me about it," she texted back.

I'd been looking over at her bunk. She had just texted me without appearing to move at all. Dang, she was a really good spy.

With Danielle on a knife's edge and no way to keep her from talking *or* to extract her, it was extra important that I get through to her. I was hoping that the time was right—she seemed vulnerable and eager to talk about her past. I just had to get her to talk to *me*, not to the world at large. With the fires nearby, the air quality was a little worse than usual. None of us wanted to compromise our singing voices, so instead of going to "the rock," we decided to sneak out and meet in our practice room. We were hoping that the counselors wouldn't be patrolling as usual because of all the smoke in the air.

Casey stayed behind to work on his song, which simplified things for me. I didn't need to be distracted while I was trying to connect with Danielle.

The Factory had packed a few high-quality masks—with the climate crisis, you never knew about the West Coast these days—and I made everyone put them on as we walked across the grass. We didn't run or even walk too fast. The smoke may have been only moderate, but I didn't want to breathe too heavily if I could help it.

As soon as we arrived, Danielle broke out the bottles and cups.

Andréa opened the curtains so the moonlight could stream in, but we kept the lights off. We didn't want to attract any counselors' attention.

"None for me," Noelani said. "I've got a one-on-one with my drum teacher first thing. I never drink when I want to be sharp."

"Actually," Andréa said, "I'm gonna pass tonight, too."

She shot me a quick glance, and I got her hint. Maybe this would be my chance to really drill down with Danielle. "More for us!" I said.

Danielle started with three shots again. Thank goodness the cups weren't see-through and the night was dark. I fake-poured three shots, putting just a dribble of liquor in each one, but then knocked them back as if they were full and made myself shudder after each one.

Then I just mirrored Danielle emotionally. When she started getting giggly, I got giggly, too.

"Oh my God, was that a bat?" Andréa asked, jumping up and looking out through the window.

"Where?" Noelani asked, swiveling her head around quickly.

"Over there!" Andréa said. "You've gotta see it. Come on!"

She grabbed Noelani's hand, and they headed outside to chase it. Andréa was so quick! What a great idea, giving me a chance for a one-on-one with Danielle.

I closed the door behind them. The air smelled a little better than it had.

"Casey sure is confident about his song," I said.

Danielle shook her head and waved her hand in front of her, as if she were shooing away a fly.

"He's sooo emo," she said. "He thinks he's having some big emotional revelation, but he's always over-the-top. Watch, it'll be some romance thing. Totally predictable."

"Yeah," I said. "Mine is on the other end. Personal, not predictable, but not really commercial, either."

"When that songwriting teacher said we needed to tell our stories for real, I didn't know what to think," Danielle said. "But I'm actually really glad I got all of that off my chest."

"Yeah," I said. "Totally."

"It was something I had never really told anyone," she said. "But it wasn't until after I said it out loud—said it when I was sober, I guess—that I really realized how much it had affected me."

"Yeah," I said. "It seems like a lot for one person to carry alone."

"Noelani says she misses Sarita, but I miss her, too," Danielle said. "She's my best friend. It was killing me not to be able to tell her this."

"Yeah," I said. "She seems so cool. But we're here for you. Me, Andréa, Noelani. I don't know about Casey."

We both laughed.

"But we girls are," I said.

"I know you are," Danielle said, and threw her arms around me and cried. "I am so glad you and Andréa are here. I can see now how alone I've been feeling because I was carrying this secret. Because my mom and I were just in this . . . like, bubble of grief or something. And now I'm coming out of it. I don't want to be trapped in there. I just— I want people, you know? More than just my mom. More than just one friend. Like, a real group. A real band. And also just . . . like . . . being the only Black girl is really hard. Especially in Hawaii, because it's, like, not all white, but there are so few Black people. And the ones that are there, so many are mixed and sort of look Native Hawaiian, so they kinda blend into the pan-Asian thing. But the brown girls like us really stick out, and that makes it hard. Like, I never realized how hard until you came along."

"We Black girls gotta stick together," I said.

Danielle scowled. "That was what my mom said. But then she didn't— She wasn't— Well, you heard it in the song."

"Yeah," I said. "But just because she failed you in a big way doesn't mean she wasn't right about Black people sticking together."

"Ugh," Danielle said. "How can someone be so wrong and so right at the same time?"

I laughed. "Moms," I said. "What can you do? You can't really fire them."

Danielle laughed, too. "Right?" she said. "I am really disappointed in you, young lady. You're fired. Go get a job as someone else's mom."

We cracked up.

"But, like, that would also be bad," she said. "Because, really, she's all I have left."

And this time she began crying for real. She put her head on my shoulder and cried hard, big sobs shaking her body.

As her tears soaked my shoulder, I crossed my fingers that this would be the breakthrough we were hoping for. I would wait until she was done crying and then suggest therapy. Maybe she would finally get in touch with her grief and that would help with her anger.

But when she wiped her eyes, I didn't get a chance to mention a therapist. "Can I show you something?" she asked.

"Sure," I said.

She reached into her wallet and pulled out a photo. "This . . . this was my dad," she said. "It's the only photo

I have. My mom got rid of all of them except the big framed photos in our living room."

In it were two people, but Danielle had her thumb over one of them. The one I could see was a smiling bald man who looked a lot like Danielle. I recognized him from the briefing materials. He had her same long, slender frame, same brown skin, same sharp eyes.

"I'm so sorry for your loss," I said. "Who's the other person?"

"His former partner," she said. "My so-called uncle. Dayvon." She took her thumb down, and it took all my spy training not to react. In the photo next to him was another man I recognized.

David.

An operative from the Factory who had helped save my life.

He had literally helped me escape one night in a rain of gunfire. *David,* I thought. *His real name is David.* But I wasn't supposed to know that.

"They . . . um . . . worked together?" I managed to ask.

"Yeah," she said. "I got this photo out of the 'box of secrets.' They were together the night my dad died. We used to be really close. But I haven't seen him in years. My mom said he's a spy, too." She put the photo away and sighed. "I'm glad I spilled the tea today."

I smiled and nodded, glad Danielle was drunk. Anyone sober could have been able to tell that my smile wasn't genuine, that I was panicked, and that I already knew who the man was.

When I got back to the cabin, I texted Jerrold. "You didn't tell me that Danielle's dad's partner was David."

He texted back: "That was strictly on a need-to-know basis. Besides, it shouldn't matter who the operative was. I hope you would work equally hard to protect anyone in our ranks."

"I would," I replied. "I just wasn't prepared. I almost lost my game face. I bungled my opportunity to mention therapy."

"Well, let me fill you in on another critical detail," he said. "David is the agent in South Carolina at Zemazin. He's been doing some labor organizing. Monty Hughes cannot get wind of anything that would connect David to espionage. He is a very dangerous man. It's urgent that Danielle NOT make it to the finals at his Northern California residence in Silicon Valley, where she and Monty might cross paths. The roads are safe again, so after tomorrow's contest, we'll have Sheila pick up Danielle. Then we'll do an assessment. If she seems the least bit unstable, we'll send them out of the country for a few months to do some follow-up. It's out of your hands at this point. Just make sure the band doesn't win."

"Copy that," I texted, then signed off.

So my work was clear. As the lead singer, I needed

to tank the contest. I couldn't help feeling that I had failed Danielle, but I was also relieved that Jerrold was going to be taking over. I didn't want David to come under any suspicion.

As for the contest, I was sorry that I wouldn't be able to sing my heart out, but it would be easier, too. I didn't need to do my best; I just needed to do my worst.

TWENTY-ONE

When Danielle sat down to lunch the next day, her eyes were shining with something new. Some sort of passion and purpose. Could a good cry do that for you? Even if you were a little drunk? I hoped so. Maybe she would pass the assessment and get to go back to Hawaii with her mom.

Casey also had a look on his face, but his expression was harder to read.

Noelani, in contrast, was jubilant. "My drum teacher thinks I have real talent!" she said. "He told me that no matter what happens with the contest, he wants me to be in his elite student intensive later this year!"

"That's amazing," Andréa said. "Congratulations!"

"Well, I have good news, too," Casey said. "I worked on my song all last night. I think it's the best I've ever written. And I think we should do it for the contest."

"Great, Casey," Noelani said. "I can't wait to hear it."

"Well, then I guess I have bad news," Danielle said. "Because I also worked on my song. And I want to use *mine* for the contest."

I felt a clutch of panic in my chest.

"The song you shared in lyric writing class?" Noelani asked.

"Yes," Danielle said. "I'm ready to tell my story."

I didn't dare look at Andréa. I just pasted on a smile and said, "Wow! An embarrassment of riches. How do we choose?"

"Yeah," Noelani said. "We've never had two songwriters before. It was always about choosing which one of Casey's songs to perform. And they were all sort of about the same type of subject, so it was easier."

"Well, we believe in democracy, right?" Andréa said. "I guess we should hear each song and vote."

"That sounds right," Noelani said.

"Okay," I said. "After lunch, let's use our practice time to listen to each of the songs, give feedback, and vote."

"Does everyone agree to that?" Andréa asked.

Everyone did. But a chill had settled over our table, and we all finished the meal in silence.

◆ ◆ ◆

Half an hour later, both of the competitors were set up and ready to share. Danielle had her keyboard, and Casey had his ukulele.

Danielle went first. She had made a few minor changes compared to what I'd heard in class, and it was an even more terrifying, cover-blowing story than before.

"My mother dealt in secrets
My mother was a spy"

As I listened, I used a technique my spy training taught me. If you have to listen to something long or boring or awkward or upsetting and you think your face might give you away, do this: put your hand under your chin and your index finger over your lips. It looks like an expression of deep listening, but it will help keep you from smiling, giggling, or frowning.

"Not the CIA, and not the FBI
Not the KGB, a different kind of lie
An army of Black people
My father was their spy
They sent him on a mission
They sent him off to die"

As she sang, Danielle sat at the keyboard, eyes

closed. She seemed to be deep in the music, deep in the story. At one point, her voice wavered like it might crack and she might start sobbing. But she finished strong.

After Danielle was done, we all clapped. I found myself trying not to throw up. An army of Black people, responsible for her father's death? We were non-violent, but if this song got any traction, that fact would get lost in the hysteria. It was a worst-case scenario coming to life.

Not only did we need to keep the song from winning—we also needed to keep the song from making it to the stage.

I turned to Andréa. Her expression told me that she completely understood the danger.

I looked over at Casey and Noelani. They both seemed moved by the song, and they were clapping enthusiastically. Casey looked a little misty-eyed.

"That's a really hard act to follow," he said, "but here goes. Keep in mind that I wrote it for Imani to sing."

If I needed to put a finger over my mouth for Danielle's song, I should have put a whole hand over my mouth for Casey's song. As near as I could tell, the song was all about me. Out of the corner of my eye, I could see Andréa and Noelani looking over at me. But I stayed stone-faced.

"I want a love like an avalanche . . ."

It was as if he had taken his cue from Noelani's talk the night before. She had explained that most girls were overwhelmed by an avalanche of romantic gestures. Well, apparently he was looking for a girl who liked that. But the song itself wasn't bad. He had clearly been working hard. The metaphors were strong, and the visual images were compelling.

After it was over, I was able to get my hands to clap politely, but I couldn't quite find my voice.

"Wow," Noelani said. "Those are both amazing songs."

"I feel really lucky that we have two options of such high quality," Andréa said. "So we have a big decision to make. Can we maybe talk about each song a little and sort of discuss strategy before we vote?"

"Great idea," I said, finally finding my voice.

Noelani began. "Danielle, I didn't get a chance to say this in class, because of the no-feedback and confidentiality rules, but I just . . . your song is so powerful. So real. I really appreciate how brave you are. And it shows. I think Imani's voice would be so great singing it. Okay, wait, we're not voting yet, but—I mean, her voice would be great for both, but I can really hear her singing about a mother-daughter situation like that, and I think it could really work."

"I love it, too," Andréa said. "I agree, ten out of ten for originality and being so personal. I guess I just wonder about relatability. Maybe we could change it just a little to make it more everygirl, you know? Like, about a family secret that was more vague, so everyone could imagine their own family there?"

I relaxed a little. Andréa was so smart.

"But remember what the lyrics teacher told us," Noelani said. "Telling your specific story is what makes it universal."

"Okay," Casey said. "Let's not get into too much back-and-forth about strategy. This was just supposed to be the feedback part. Do you all have any feedback for me?"

"Sure," Noelani said. "You're right, Casey. This is your best song yet."

"Yeah," Andréa said. "The metaphors about weather and nature really make it next-level."

I realized that Danielle likely wasn't going to comment on her competition. So I should probably say something. But what could I say?

"As a vocalist," I said, "I loved the melody. I could really see myself going in with some of the phrasing. Like, you held some notes so long, it would give me a chance to do some flourishes and stuff. I think it could be a real crowd-pleaser."

"Okay," Noelani said. "We're not strategizing yet."

"Bottom line," Andréa said. "They're both really good. Any more feedback for either one before we start to strategize?"

We sat for a moment, and no one spoke.

"You know," I said, "I really need a chance to process. It was a lot of amazing work. Can we come back together after dinner and check in about it?"

"Yes," Noelani said. "That's a great idea."

"This is a nightmare," I said to Andréa as we headed to dinner. "I should never have pushed so hard for Danielle to come to camp. I'm in way over my head. Now it could be the worst of all worlds. The Factory gets exposed, the agent's cover gets blown, *and* Danielle gets extracted."

"Don't panic," Andréa said. "We still have time to figure something out. If we pick Danielle's song, we could try to influence the lyrics. Maybe get her to tone it down a bit? I think we could make a case for her taking out a lot of the operation specifics. What teenager can relate to that?"

"That's good," I said. "We still have options."

"Yes!" Andréa said. "We have options. We have each other. And we have a good team to support us."

"Okay," I said. "Plan A is to get her to tone the lyrics way down. Plan B is to go with Casey's song."

"Copy that," Andréa said.

I was feeling a little bit of relief. We were far from being out of the woods, but I had a partner, a team, and a plan with a contingency plan.

Things were tense at the table with the band, but dinner was appealing for once. Pizza. It's hard to wreck pizza. I had just taken a bite when the camp director rang a chime to get everyone's attention.

"I have an exciting announcement," she chirped. "Even the darkest of clouds has a silver lining. Our new sponsor, Monty Hughes, has a mountain home nearby. He was supposed to go to Paris this week, but with the fires, he's stayed in the area. And that's a lucky break for us, because he decided to come to our final concert!"

I nearly choked on the pizza. At the last second, I opened my mouth in what I was hoping was a *wow!* smile. Andréa smiled back, but her face also looked strained. Hopefully, no one noticed. Jerrold had said Monty Hughes was exactly the worst-case-scenario person to hear the song. If we didn't figure something out ASAP, we might need to get that emergency helicopter and literally kidnap Danielle to get her out of this camp.

TWENTY-TWO

The air was a little better again, so our group reconvened at the stone circle by the pond. "Okay," Noelani said. "Let's talk strategy."

"Obviously, I'm biased," Danielle said. "But people keep telling us that we need to stand out. I think my song really will. It's different from what people expect. And it's from the heart. People will feel that. I think we should go with mine."

Andréa nodded slowly. "I can really see that," she said. "But I also think it's a risk. Yes, young people will identify with that sense of betrayal from their parents. I think we've all had some version of our parents not telling us something. But the judges are adults. I don't think they'll feel it as strongly. I would consider supporting it if we changed the lyrics a little to be more relatable—like I said before. I just think that, otherwise, yeah, it'll stand out, but I just don't think it has the mass appeal."

"I agree," I said. "I love it, Danielle. I think it's so powerful. But I agree about it not having mass appeal. I would also love to see a new version with more relatable lyrics."

Danielle was shaking her head. "I feel like this is the moment where bands lose their identity. They miss their chance to be something new and big by trying to be the same old mediocre."

"You're calling my song mediocre?" Casey asked.

"I'm sorry," Danielle said. "I didn't mean it like that. I mean . . . safe. I would rather take a risk on something more edgy to really stand out. I think your song is great, Casey, but I think that a love song is safe."

"Well, I didn't enter this contest to make a statement about just one person's life," he said. "Don't get me wrong—I'd love to do your song as part of a full set. But I don't think it's the right choice for a contest where we only get one shot. Bottom line, *I* want to win."

Noelani jumped in. "All of us want to win, Casey."

"And I don't think Danielle's song is the vehicle to win," he said. "Especially if she won't accept any changes. There's a compromise here. And if she won't compromise, then it's more about her than it is about the whole band."

"So it's getting to be a big back-and-forth," Andréa said. "I think we should vote."

"Fine," Danielle said. "I vote for my song."

"Me, too," Noelani said.

"I vote for my song," Casey said.

"And you both obviously agree with him," Danielle said, looking at us angrily.

Andréa and I looked at each other. Why couldn't Danielle be a little more flexible? If she would just make a few changes, everything would be okay. I didn't want to vote for Casey's song. I didn't want to *sing* Casey's song. I also didn't want to lose my connection with Danielle, especially since she had been opening up to me earlier. I had been this close to broaching the subject of therapy, which was her best chance to not have her life blown up . . . again. But if I voted for Danielle, she would reveal her family's story in front of Monty Hughes. There was no way I could let that happen.

"I don't think you understand," Andréa said. "Imani and I like both songs." She turned to me. "Am I right?"

"Yeah," I said. "For sure. Danielle's song is my first choice if we get a new version with more relatable lyrics."

"So it's really up to *you*," Andréa went on, looking directly at Danielle. "We're both into your song if you're willing to make it more relatable."

"Exactly," I said. "So, Danielle, I think *you* really have the deciding vote. What are *you* willing to do?"

"No," Danielle said angrily. "It's like the moment I open up my mouth, everyone's trying to shut it again.

I'm not going to compromise. I'd rather sing Casey's stupid love song than water down mine. Forget it!"

She threw down her notebook and stormed out.

"Stupid?" Casey yelled after her. "My song is not stupid!"

I went to follow her, but Noelani stopped me. "Let me go after her," she said, her voice gentle. "I don't think she wants to hear from you right now." She headed out the door.

"Oh my God," Casey said. "You all don't know how long I was encouraging Danielle to sing and write and whatever. For months! And she was always, like, *No, I can't.* And so I had to do all the work. All the writing. All the singing. And now she's acting like I'm her enemy. No freaking appreciation." He started to leave, too.

At the door, he turned around. "If Danielle comes back, tell her I said, 'You're welcome.'"

And then we heard his footsteps receding down the path.

"Ugh," I said. "Could that have gone worse?"

"Definitely," Andréa said. "Two big wins. First, Danielle isn't going to do her song by popular vote. And second, we didn't vote against her song; we let her know we were on her side. I mean, it certainly could have gone better, but only if Danielle had made a different choice. Given that she was determined to sing her song her way, I think that went as well as possible."

"Okay," I said. "I'll try to keep your positive attitude as I call it in to HQ." I began to pull my secret cell phone out of my little backpack.

"Let me do it," Andréa said. "You should be available in case Danielle wants to talk."

I agreed. I went out and sat right in the center of the field. I didn't see Danielle at all before dinner. And when we got to dinner, she definitely didn't want to talk.

The whole next day, Danielle was surly during rehearsals. She didn't act like a bandleader, as she had in the past. Instead, Noelani counted us off for each of the rehearsals. We played Casey's song probably a hundred times.

I tried to catch Danielle's eye, but she was like a musical robot. She came in, played the keyboard, and left.

The rest of us tried not to let it kill our enthusiasm. Because other than her bad attitude, the song was sounding really good.

TWENTY-THREE

In August, the sun sets late in Oregon. It was nine in the evening when we all filed in for the final contest. The smell of smoke had diminished, and I had never been so grateful for breathable air—something I had always just taken for granted.

The competition was being held at the camp amphitheater. Even though it was outside, it was set up like a real stage. They had a full lighting grid and a state-of-the-art sound system. And of course, they had a skybox set up so that the camp's creepy benefactor, Monty Hughes, could look down on all of us.

There were three judges, as well as a few music industry adults who happened to live on the right side of the closed-off roads.

We had studied up on the judges, what they liked and didn't like, but when we got to the contest stage, the camp director explained that the winner was going to be the one who got the most applause.

"So at the end of the day, it's a popularity contest?" Noelani asked as our group gathered in one corner to warm up.

"It always is," Casey said.

"Just say it," Danielle said. "Just say it. 'Thank goodness we picked my song. There's no way that your spy song ever would have won.'"

"What?" Casey said. "No. That's not what I'm saying. I'm saying that it's always rigged against *us*, Danielle. Against the brown kids. Especially the Black kids. They expect us to be gangsta rappers. And if we're not, they're disappointed. But if we are, it's not in good taste. Basically, they always want Taylor Swift more than they want Solange Knowles. Shoot, even more than they want Beyoncé."

"Look, guys," Noelani said. "Let's focus on winning this thing. What did we say we were gonna do when we got here? Get into the zone. Let's do our breathing. Let's warm up. Let's stay on task."

"Sounds good," Andréa said.

So for the next half hour, no sounds came from our band members other than inhales and exhales, and the wordless melodies of vocal warm-ups.

Once the warm-up period was over and we had gotten into our costumes, we all settled in our seats in the amphitheater. Then the camp director walked to the stage to introduce the contest sponsor, the heels of her business shoes sinking into the dirt. Her entire outfit looked ridiculous in the context of the amphitheater.

"Monty is about to speak," she said. "I hope you all appreciate what an honor it is to be addressed by such an entrepreneurial genius."

Ugh. Like we were about to hear the voice of God.

But I was a spy, so I nodded and pasted a smile on my face, as if I were just as excited as she was.

Monty Hughes stepped up to the mic. He was maybe in his fifties, gray at the temples, and trying too hard for a guy-next-door vibe, in khakis and a polo shirt.

He could have been the father of the white guy at the audition who had quizzed me about hip-hop. He was all the braggadocio but none of the bars. He just boasted, without any music or wordplay to his recitation. His talk was just about the ages at which he had made his first million, billion, when this or that company went public. I wish I could have said it was just boring. In truth, it was offensive. He talked about the charities he had built, but really he talked about how they allowed him to keep from paying taxes and to win honors and accolades and ultimately make even more money.

I thought of his employees, some unable to feed their families, some unable to pay their medical bills, some just unable to go to the bathroom during a ten-hour shift.

He instructed us campers to be hypercompetitive,

pushing us to prepare for success in the commercial music industry, which is "dog-eat-dog."

I don't know what I would have done without Andréa. She and I kept perfectly straight faces but nudged and elbowed each other with every offensive thing he said. Like when he referred to "the wilds of Mexico" and a project "all the way over in Africa."

She passed me a note.

He says he's a self-made man, but didn't his dad give him a million dollars to start his first company?

I kept my face blank as I wrote back:

Which failed and he got a half million to start his second company.

"I never got a handout," Monty Hughes was saying. "I paid back every cent my father gave me. It wasn't a gift or even a loan. It was an investment."

On the other side of me, Noelani drew a picture of a frowny face with its head on fire.

Only rich guys get someone to "invest" in them when they haven't proven anything!

I rolled my eyes.

Not true—He had proven he could lose a million dollars.

I felt Noelani beside me trying to stifle a laugh.

After a while, the combination of nerves for the contest, anxiety about the spy mission, and sheer nauseating outrage at Monty Hughes's pompousness was making me want to scream. I had to distract myself. I started tinkering with lyrics to another song I began composing in my head, "Rich Boy":

isn't it a little funny
how you succeeded on your daddy's money
taking every advantage you can
then proclaiming to be a "self-made man" . . .

Finally, he shut up and they announced the order for the contest. We were up fifth. The first three bands had also gone safe. A breakup song, a love song, and a bland "Believe in yourself!" anthem.

And then, the fourth group got up, and I finally got excited. They were called "Total Futuration," and not only was their song about the climate crisis, but also they could really sing. The most unexpected part of the song was that it wasn't just sad or angry—it was also fiercely hopeful.

"Snap out of your trance
We still have a chance

Our species cannot fail
If we make these changes at scale"

As the song built to a climax, I started feeling like I didn't even want to continue with the assignment; I wanted to run back home and join a group that was working to solve the climate crisis.

But what I didn't expect was the audience response. They went wild. It was a gathering of teenagers who had grown up in the shadow of apocalypse, who had learned in science class that we were inheriting a dying planet. We were all so glad to hear that it might not be true, and that we could do something about it. The industry professionals seemed to love the song, too.

Even in the open-air amphitheater, without walls or a ceiling to contain us, we roared with an intensity that I hadn't imagined possible.

The judges were grinning. One woman was wiping her eyes.

And I felt so relieved. That was it. They had definitely won. Mission accomplished. At least for now. No way Flex Five was going to the finals.

Then it was our turn. We got up to do "Avalanche," and I had to remember that even though we had no chance of winning the contest, we had already won this round: we were doing a song that was *not* Danielle's in front of Monty Hughes and all these people.

And with the knowledge that Total Futuration had

knocked it out of the park, I could relax and sing my best. It was my last chance, and I wanted to enjoy it. And the song did sound great. The band was on point, and I finished really strong.

At the end, the applause was huge—not as big as for the climate band but bigger than any of the previous bands.

When we got offstage, we were all grinning. Even Danielle's scowl had turned into the shadow of a smile. Win or lose, it had felt great to perform so well—even to her. The spy in me was glad that someone else would beat us, but the singer in me was excited for my great performance.

And even better, whatever the next challenge would be, it wasn't my call. I hadn't fully succeeded at the mission, but I had done a good job, and I could be proud of my work. Andréa and I made eye contact, and I could tell she felt the same way. But then she looked out at the next band and furrowed her brow. Right. We were supposed to look crestfallen or jealous or mad. I fixed my face and waited for the judges' decision.

It felt like an eternity as the rest of the bands played. I picked at my nails. I had on the same outfit as the previous competition, and my wig itched. As soon as the winner was announced, I was planning to corner Danielle to try to have a heart-to-heart with her, without all the pressure of the competition to get in our way. I was ready to get the good news and face the music.

TWENTY-FOUR

After the final band, Monty Hughes stepped onto the stage. I hadn't seen him come down from the skybox. He had such pale skin and dark hair, and the intel on him said his business was basically bloodsucking—I wondered if maybe he'd turned into a bat and flown.

"I have good news," he said. "The roads are open and everyone will be leaving tomorrow, including our winners, who will go to Silicon Valley for the next round!"

All the participants were sitting in jittery anticipation.

"Congratulations to all the bands," he went on. "I just want a round of applause for every single young musician who was up here today. This is what it's all about. We do it for the kids.

"But we also want to give you children a real

education about the music industry, which is why some of you may be a bit surprised here. I know the winner is determined by audience applause, but there's also a clause in the rules that states that the winning song needs to be on-brand for any corporate sponsor. And the group that *both* got the most applause *and* is on-brand for Hughes Industries is . . . Flex Five!"

I had just fixed my face to look disappointed, expecting that inside I would be elated. Now, suddenly, I had to fix my face to look overjoyed when I was . . . what was I? Shocked. How could he change the rules like that?

I was also mad. How could saving the planet not be "on-brand"?

But worst of all, we weren't done? Sheila wouldn't be picking up Danielle, so we'd have to do an emergency extraction? Or, worse yet, if we couldn't pull that off, we'd have to figure out how to protect the Factory secrets in the media spotlight next to Sound Cake?

The other members of the band looked as shocked as I did. I thought maybe they'd be happy that we won, but we all knew that our win was a sham. We were ushered onto the stage, and Monty handed us certificates. The applause was polite but not at all thunderous. Thank goodness we weren't actually allowed to say anything. I have no idea what any of us would have said.

After we got offstage, the concert wrapped up with

some logistical announcements. Camp was ending the next day, and everyone was going home. Everyone except us, of course. We were going to Monty Hughes's mansion in Silicon Valley for the finals, with a special appearance by Sound Cake, who had an Instagram following of seventy-five million people. But we would never make it that far, I reassured myself. The Factory would definitely pull Danielle out, rather than risk that she spill anything.

Casey came over and put his arm around me. "We did it," he said. "Our song won."

"Yeah," I said. "I can hardly believe it."

"I can," he said. "Love always triumphs in the end."

"You mean love *songs* always triumph," I said.

"No," he said, "I mean love." He looked at me seriously. "Imani, I've watched you sing that song a hundred times. I know this feeling has been building between us."

"This what?" I asked.

"You looked right into my eyes tonight when you sang 'bring on the avalanche,'" he said.

"We were onstage, Casey," I said, "singing harmonies. I was making sure we were in time together."

"So what are you saying?" he asked.

I took a deep breath. "I've always been saying the same thing, Casey," I said. "I want to keep this professional." Good. I had let him down easy. After all, I was a spy, and he was an important person in the operation.

And I had no idea what would happen after they extracted Danielle. Would the rest of the band do the contest without her? The song could still work without a keyboard. Either way, I did need a good professional relationship with Casey.

He didn't look as upset as I imagined he would. "Okay," he said, "I guess I should have waited until after the finals to say anything. If you want to keep it all about implication and innuendo until then, I'm good with that. So yeah," he said, "let's keep it *professional*." And he winked as he said the final word.

Wait—what? "No," I said. "I don't want to keep it . . ." What was happening? Why wasn't he hearing my no?

"Casey, there *is* no implication or innuendo," I tried.

"Oh, come on," he said, winking at me again.

"Seriously," I said, getting flustered. "I want to keep it professional because I don't like you like that. I don't."

I had sort of just blurted it out. It hadn't sounded as smooth and gentle as I had hoped.

"Excuse me?" he asked flatly. Suddenly, all the winking was gone.

"No," I said. "Actually, the idea that the song is somehow about me makes me really uncomfortable."

"Oh, *now* you're saying it makes you uncomfortable?" he asked. "After you've sung it to me over a hundred times?"

"Sung it *to* you?" I asked, suddenly angry. "What

are you even talking about? I was singing in a *contest*, trying to *win*. Playing a role. It's all fake." I snatched off the wig. "The hair, the eyelashes, the romantic vibe. I'm a *vocalist*. It's like what they said at the beginning: music is about making other people feel something. I was trying to make the audience feel something."

"Are you sure you weren't trying to make *me* feel something?" he asked.

I flashed back to a couple of our . . . moments. I *had* sort of felt something. And maybe it could have grown into something more. But now he was using the word "love"? He hadn't even said he liked me, let alone asked if I liked him.

Trying to make him feel something? He was making it seem like I had led him on. What the hell was he talking about?

"No," I said, completely furious, "I never tried to make you feel anything. *You* were trying to make *me* feel something. That whole song was you putting words into my mouth. You thought if I sang them over and over that I would just fall in line with your plan? Forget it."

I threw the wig at him and stormed off.

Andréa was walking toward me, eyes wide. And then it hit me. I was a spy. I had totally lost control.

As we passed each other, she muttered, "Go cool off. I'll talk to Casey."

I nodded. What had I just done?

Outside our cabin, I sort of paced back and forth. Noelani came and sat on the porch swing.

"Bittersweet, right?" she said. "The climate song should have won. Especially after the hurricane and all the wildfires here. Feels kind of like we won at the expense of the planet."

I just nodded.

"I thought that winning would feel great, but everything is messed up," Noelani said. "Danielle is still pissed about the song. What else is new, though, right? I don't know. I just wish Sarita were here. She really has a way of talking her down. It's getting exhausting."

I couldn't just wait there anymore. Noelani and I agreed to go find the other band members to fill out the paperwork for the final competition. She went in search of Danielle. I went in search of Andréa, who would be able to update me on Casey. But I didn't want to show up when they were still talking, so instead of walking off in search of them, I sent Andréa a text message. I could just imagine her chatting with Casey and having her phone buzz silently against her calf.

Five minutes later, I got a text. She would be coming to the cabin with Casey in about fifteen minutes. Was that good? Bad? Before they arrived, Danielle and Noelani showed up.

"Just think," Noelani was saying as Danielle scowled, "you did this to spend a little time away from your mom this summer. Now it'll be double the time, with an amazing opportunity to get into the music industry."

I felt a buzz against my leg, but there was no way to answer it discreetly.

"I need to grab something out of the cabin," I said.

"Wait," Noelani said. "Here come Andréa and Casey."

Sure enough, they were walking toward us across the lawn. Casey looked even more furious than before. I wondered what Andréa had said to him.

"Is that the band roster?" Casey asked, coming up and gesturing to the clipboard in Noelani's hand. "Does it include the song we're playing?"

"Oh my God, Casey," Danielle said. "Will you give it a rest with the song already?"

"Scratch it out," Casey said. "I want Danielle's song."

"What?!" Andréa and I said in unison. Danielle's jaw dropped open.

"I just don't even care about love songs anymore," Casey said. "I can't stand to play it one more time."

"That's nuts," Noelani said. "It was literally our winning song."

"Danielle's song is better," he insisted. "We should do that one."

"With Sound Cake?" Andréa asked. "Literally the K-pop love song group? I thought you wanted to win."

"But we didn't win," Danielle said, looking determined. "The climate song won. It's just that Monty

Hughes thought it wasn't 'on-brand.' But he's not judging the final contest, and he won't feel that way about my song anyway. Plus, in a sea of love songs, it's really gonna stand out. I think Casey's right. I think it's our best shot."

"Sounds good to me," Casey said. "And anyway, I'm not playing the other song."

"Is this about what I said earlier?" I asked.

He turned to me with raised eyebrows. "Look, Imani," he said. "After you shared your feelings for me, I just don't feel comfortable playing that song. I wish you could keep it more professional."

Um . . . what?! He was acting like *I* was the one with feelings for *him*?! "You wish—? You think—?" I stammered. I couldn't get myself together.

Noelani was shaking her head with an eye roll. Clearly, she knew exactly what was really going on.

"Casey, I don't think—"

"Let's do it," Danielle said. "And you know what? I want to sing lead. I'm ready to sing my song."

"Wait a minute," Noelani said.

"I agree!" Casey said. "That's two votes. This is a democracy, remember? Last time Danielle and Noelani voted for Danielle's song. Well, I'm changing my vote. That makes three for Danielle. Unless someone else is changing their vote." He turned to Noelani.

"I don't—" she began, looking from Danielle to me and Andréa.

"Are you changing or not?" Danielle asked.

"No, but—" Noelani tried again.

"Isn't there supposed to be some discussion before a vote?" Andréa asked.

"I just think—" Noelani began.

"It was already voted on," Casey said.

"Then the motion passes," Danielle said. "We're doing my song."

"Wait—" Noelani began, but Casey interrupted her.

"I want to make another motion," he said. "I say we remove Imani from the group."

"What?" This time it was Andréa, Noelani, and me in unison.

"I second the motion," Danielle said. "Imani was singing lead, but if I'm going to sing—and I am—what does she really add?"

"Casey, stop and think about this for a minute," said Andréa.

"Think about what?" he asked. "She's not really a member of the band. She just joined in San Diego. Come to think about it, I'm not sure that we need you anymore, either."

"But Andréa plays guitar," Noelani said.

"She's really just the sub for Sarita," Casey said. "And I feel like she's been undermining this group all along. We can replace her in the finals. I'm sure the contest can make that happen."

"I'm not okay with this," Noelani said.

“Look,” Andréa said. “It’s been a really emotional night. Tempers are running high. I’m going to decide not to take this personally, and I hope Imani can do the same. Let’s just put all our names on the band roster and sleep on it. We can discuss it again in the morning when we have cooler heads.”

“Nope,” Casey said. “My mind is made up.” He turned to Danielle and Noelani. “If they don’t leave the band, I’ll leave the band.”

“Me too,” Danielle said standing next to Casey. “Either they go or we go.”

“Danielle,” Noelani said, “don’t do this.”

“I’m not doing anything,” she said. “I’m going to bed. You fill out the roster form however you like. But if their names are on it, I’m not going to Silicon Valley. And that’s final.”

And with that, she spun on her heel and went into the cabin.

“What she said,” Casey hissed at us, and strode off toward the guys’ cabins.

TWENTY-FIVE

For a second, we just stood there, stunned.

"What are we gonna do?" I asked Noelani.

"I don't think we have a choice," she said.

"You're gonna let them kick us out?" Andréa asked.

"What's the other option?" Noelani asked. "If we put down your names, we'll lose either Casey or Danielle or both. They're the songwriters. Either way, we can't do it without them."

Andréa opened her mouth to argue, but I jumped in.

"Okay," I said, thinking quickly. "I totally understand the spot you're in. Come on, Andréa, let's be gracious about this. We've had a good run. But we were always the outsiders. The band's gotta do what the band's gotta do."

"Thank you so much," Noelani said. "Lemme go

turn in this band roster. I'll check in with Danielle when I get back. I'm really sorry. It was great working with both of you."

"It's not your fault," I said. "I get it."

Noelani hugged us both and then went to drop off the roster.

"You didn't think it was worth fighting to keep us in the band?" Andréa asked.

"I didn't think it was a fight we could win," I said. "And I don't think it matters, anyway. They're not going to make it to Silicon Valley, not if there's a chance they're going to play that song. We need to go to the team and get instructions for their extraction plan."

"Copy that," she said.

We bumped fists a bit dejectedly.

"I'll go find a quiet spot to call in," I said.

I circled back behind the cabin. Usually, it would be lights-out by now, but they were allowing us another hour to pack and say a first round of goodbyes. We would leave in the morning after breakfast.

But as I came around the corner of the cabin, I heard music—an unexpectedly familiar song.

Danielle was singing. She had her keyboard set up and was sitting on a tree stump, playing her song.

"You minded everyone's business but your own
You were blinded by your profession
And you left me all alone"

I couldn't deny it: the song was beautiful. Danielle had found her voice and was singing her heart out. With that much passion behind it, the song did have the potential to win.

I was more worried than I had been at any time during the mission. Danielle was armed with an incredible voice and actionable intel about the Factory, and she was headed to a massive concert that would be live streamed publicly to millions. The security risk had never been greater.

Since I couldn't call without drawing attention to myself, I sent a message to the Factory saying as much. I got a message back saying that I should go to bed and do my best to sleep. We would receive instructions in the morning on how to proceed.

So I did as I was told—at least part of it. I went to bed, and I was under the covers before either Danielle or Noelani got back.

But I couldn't follow the second part of my instructions. I lay in bed for hours without falling asleep. And then I made a big mistake—I started scrolling on my phone. I looked up the latest news about Monty Hughes. He was in hot water for illegal strikebreaking tactics in South Carolina.

"Actually," he said to the press, "I'm the real victim here. There are outside agitators coming to my factories and stirring up trouble. I've received multiple awards in South Carolina for having a top-notch workplace. But mark my words. I'm going to find these outside agitators, and I'm going to expose them and prosecute them to the fullest extent of the law."

Then I read a piece from the perspective of the South Carolina unionizing efforts. They said that a leak from Hughes's team told them that he was having explosive fits of rage, referring to "secret underground terrorist groups" and vowing to devote his resources to tracking them down and doxing them. Apparently, he had several corporate spies infiltrating the union. So he had a counterintelligence program going? Was David going to be okay?

I lay in bed for a long time, my heart beating fast. I tried texting Andréa. "R u awake?" But it seemed like she was smart enough not to doomscroll on her phone at two a.m. and had probably fallen asleep.

At some point, I did manage to doze off, but I think I dreamed that Danielle was onstage singing a song of rage to my parents, who were back in Georgia. The two of them fell into murky water, where Monty Hughes tied Zemazin package after package onto them until they both went under.

TWENTY-SIX

I arrived at breakfast still rattled and bleary-eyed. The only message we had gotten said "Stand by." We still hadn't received instructions on what the plan would be.

The morning was cold and overcast, matching the energy of most of the young musicians. The whole camp had a sort of funereal air. Most people were bummed because they had lost. Andréa and I were bummed, too—ostensibly because we'd been kicked out of the group, but really because we were worried about the mission. Noelani was upset because her band had broken up, and Casey was upset because—apparently—he'd decided to believe that my heart was in the words that he had given me to sing, even though I'd never said them on my own. And I hoped that somewhere, deep inside, he was upset because he had been such a self-centered jerk.

In contrast to everyone else, Danielle was unreadable. Not happy. Not sad. Not angry. Her face was sort of aggressively blank.

Most of the kids were going in buses to the Portland Airport. The winning band got a charter van to Silicon Valley, and we were gonna make a detour to the San Francisco Airport so that Andréa and I could be dropped off.

It was almost time to get in the van when I felt a buzz at my ankle. I looked up at the van driver.

"Hold on," I said. "I need to go to the bathroom."

"Me too," Andréa said, and we headed to the closest restroom, which was inside the dining hall.

"Did you get a message?" I asked.

She shook her head. "You'll need to brief me."

We went into separate stalls, and I looked at my phone.

After I came out, I carefully looked in the other two stalls to make sure the bathroom was empty.

"So?" Andréa asked.

"It's just as we expected," I reported. "They said the risk is too great. They have to keep Danielle out of that spotlight. If she doesn't get to the Silicon Valley concert in time to check in, she'll be disqualified. They're gonna stage a carjacking on a rural part of the road on the way down, and it will delay Danielle for a couple of hours, enough to keep her off the big finals stage."

"So they're gonna handle it all?" she asked. "Then what's our job?"

"I guess just to look scared when the carjackers come," I said. "And not to use our hand-to-hand combat training to beat them."

"I'll try to keep that in mind," Andréa said. "Sometimes my lightning-fast reflexes just kick in." She kicked the air.

I gave a weak laugh as we walked back to the van.

On the one hand, I was genuinely relieved that the adults were taking over. But on the other hand, I sort of felt like we had failed.

In the parking lot, they were just finishing loading up all our stuff onto the transportation.

As the other bands boarded their buses, I spotted Total Futuration, the climate band.

I turned to Andréa. "I really want to tell them I appreciate them for their song."

"Great idea," Andréa said. "Let's go."

"Yeah," I said. "But I'm worried that they might be mad at us for winning."

"There's only one way to find out," Andréa said, and took my arm, pulling me toward them.

The lead singer was a young Tongan woman, wearing a T-shirt that said ONLY HUMANS CAN STOP SEA LEVEL RISE.

"Hey," I said. "Thank you so much for your song—for all your work."

I was steeled for her to have an attitude, but she lit up. "Yeah," she said, "I really appreciate that." She turned to Andréa. "And I saw you had on a Puerto Rico T-shirt. Are you Boricua?"

Andréa nodded. "On my mom's side. Hurricane Maria really opened my eyes about climate. Is your song online?"

"Absolutely," the singer said, and fished in her pocket. "Here's a flyer for our music page. That's just one of our climate songs. We have a collaboration with a reggaeton group out of Arecibo that I think you would love." She handed one to each of us as she moved up the bus steps.

"My socials are on there, too," she said before she disappeared into the bus. "Be in touch!"

We waved goodbye to her and walked across the parking lot to our little van.

But before any of us in Flex Five could climb aboard, Monty Hughes walked over and shook each of our hands. I kind of wanted to put my hands behind my back, but there was no way to do that without drawing attention to myself. When we shook, his hand was cold—further reinforcing my vampire theory.

"Great work," he said. "Good luck in the finals!" Apparently, no one had told him that two of us wouldn't be participating.

Andréa and I sat in the back of the van. Danielle and Noelani sat in the middle, and Casey sat up front, near the driver.

The ride became more and more awkward as we drove. Everyone had gotten their phones back, so each band member was hunkered down looking at their own screen.

After a few hours, as we drove down a secluded two-lane highway, Andréa and I were finally able to message each other.

"Do you see that sedan that's been following us?" I asked.

"Charcoal gray," she said. "Could that be the team?"

"I think so," I said.

Then we were quiet for a while, keeping an eye on the sedan.

I watched the trees fly by, flashes of light and darker green, with the rusty-brown trunks of the redwoods. In the distance, we saw blackened hills where the fire had roared through.

In several miles, there was a passing lane, and the sedan sped by us. A few minutes later, we came around a curve and saw the sedan in front of us. The next thing we knew, it disappeared again and we heard a squeal of brakes up ahead.

Our driver slowed down, and when we came around the next curve, we saw the sedan had stopped. In front of it was a pile of rocks that had ostensibly fallen from the side of the mountain next to the road. At least, I figured that's what it was supposed to look like.

Our driver stopped behind the sedan. There was a man standing outside the car—tall, with dark hair, racially ambiguous. I didn't recognize him.

I had assumed that this was the carjacking spot, but then again, maybe it was just a real rockfall? Some of the trees on the hill above had fire damage. Even before the fires, all the heat and drought from the climate crisis meant that trees were dying or becoming more brittle. There was more erosion, and genuine rockslides were becoming more frequent. Fires just accelerated what was already happening.

The other teens looked up at the rockfall and groaned, but then they went back to their screens. Andréa and I kept our eyes trained on the man and the sedan.

Our driver, an older Asian guy, got out of the van, and the guy from the sedan came over to him. We could hear their conversation through the windows.

"Did you take the keys out with you?" he asked our driver. "You wouldn't want to leave them in the car with all those kids."

"I've got 'em right here," the driver said.

"Not anymore," the guy said—and grabbed the keys.

Noelani gasped. Apparently, she had been paying

attention. Casey's and Danielle's heads popped up to see what was going on.

"What the—?" our driver began. But he stopped talking, and we saw a gun in the guy's hand.

"Oh God, oh God, oh God," Noelani was saying.

"We don't want any trouble," the carjacker said. "We just want the van. Make the kids come out with their hands up, and nobody gets hurt."

Even though I knew the carjacking was fake, and the gun was probably fake, too, I felt scared anyway. I didn't have to pretend. We marched out of the van, all of us with our hands up.

Casey was next to me, sort of putting his body between me and the carjacker. Was he trying to protect me? That was ridiculous. I was taller than him by an inch and wider than him by a few inches.

"Please," the driver said. "Can the kids just get their stuff?"

"Sorry for the inconvenience," the carjacker said.

As he turned to board our van, Danielle leaped forward.

"No!" I yelled, but it was too late. She grabbed the carjacker around the waist, and he spun around. Danielle ducked out of the immediate range of the gun.

It was a move I knew well. I had forgotten that she'd taken self-defense.

Suddenly, the carjacker's sedan started up. There

must have been a second person in there we couldn't see, thanks to heavily tinted windows.

The car drove toward Danielle, and she leaped out of the way, rolled across the lane of traffic to the outer edge of the road, and took off running.

I tried to leap forward—to go after her—but Casey leaned his body back against me, maybe trying to protect me once again. I was sort of pinned to the side of the mountain for a moment. Andréa also tried to jump in, but the van was starting up, and she couldn't chase Danielle without risking getting run over.

As the van drove off, we all stepped away from the mountain. We looked around desperately for Danielle, but she had disappeared into the thick trees by the side of the road.

TWENTY-SEVEN

Oh my God," Noelani said. "What do we do now?"

"I need to call in to my dispatcher," the driver said.

"We need to find Danielle," I said.

"Let's go look for her," Andréa said.

There wasn't any cell service on this part of the road, so we split up and agreed to meet back in half an hour. Andréa and I went down the road in one direction, and Casey, Noelani, and the driver went in another.

"Freaking Casey," I said. "I could have caught her if he hadn't made such a show of 'protecting' me. I swear, that guy is the bane of my existence."

"I should have been bolder," Andréa said. "I should have stayed closer to her."

I sighed. "We did our best," I said. "Both of us."

We looked for about half an hour. We saw amazing, majestic redwoods. We saw oak trees. We saw multiple blackened hillsides at the horizon where the fire had been. We even saw a coyote and a bunch of deer. But no Danielle.

The whole time, Andréa and I were trying to get a cell signal. Apparently, we had been carjacked on a section of the road where the signal was bad, which would have been perfect if only Danielle hadn't run away. We kept searching, both for her and for any reception on our phones. It was another half hour before we found a spot where we had a signal. I called in the update to our team. It took forever, because I couldn't yell out our spy business, and half the time they couldn't hear me. Eventually, I messaged the sensitive parts, and we had the conversation half in talk, half in text.

We trudged back to the spot where we'd been carjacked. As we rounded the corner, we saw Noelani and Casey. They looked much happier than we were.

"Did you find her?" Andréa asked.

Noelani shook her head. "No, but the carjackers dumped all our stuff farther down the road in a turnout: backpacks, sleeping bags, instruments, everything. The driver's waiting down there."

"That's good," Andréa said. But I wasn't sure what was going to happen next.

Fortunately for us, the camp organizers didn't have

another van, so they picked us up in two separate cars. It took a while to arrange for the rides, and when they showed up, Andréa and I sort of drifted to one car, and Noelani, Casey, and the driver went to the other.

After Andréa and I had belted ourselves in, the driver of our car turned back to us.

"The Factory sent me," she said. "You can speak freely."

I heaved a sigh of relief.

"Gracias a Dios," Andréa said. "Is there an update?"

"Jerrold should be calling any moment," she said.

On one side of the car, trees flashed past, and on the other was just the side of the mountain. It was the same road as before, but it felt different. On the one hand, I was not looking forward to checking in now that we had lost Danielle. But on the other hand, I felt safer and more grounded knowing that I was back with my Factory team.

And as we rounded the next curve, the phone rang.

Jerrold's voice came through strong and clear: "Amani, Andréa," he began, "I just want to tell you not to take it too hard. You all did great work. In some ways, this was your most difficult mission yet. You've hit every conceivable type of setback, but you kept trying, and we're still trying."

"Any sign of Danielle?" Andréa asked.

"Unfortunately, no," he said. "Her cell was on briefly,

but now it's off. We have no idea where she is."

"Could she be on a bus to Silicon Valley?" Andréa asked. "Or a train? Or plane?"

"We have all the train and bus stations staked out," he said. "We expect that she may have hitched a ride."

"That's so dangerous," I said.

"It is," Jerrold said. "But she has self-defense skills, and she managed to escape from a carjacker. We have to hope she's safe. And the hitchhiking theory has advantages for us. If she's hitching rides from Oregon to Silicon Valley, chances are she won't be able to get to the concert on time. Everyone has to be there to check in by the deadline or else they won't be able to perform."

"Okay, good," I said. "Fingers crossed for that outcome: Danielle is safe but gets disqualified. What time is the deadline?"

"In eight hours," he said. "The carjacking slowed things down enough that Casey and Noelani will barely make it, even going straight there. If Danielle has to find rides on top of that, there's no way she'll get there in time."

Eight hours.

And then there was nothing to do but wait. For the first time in days, Andréa and I didn't have to keep our cover. We could truly relax. And as the car purred down the highway, all the late nights and contest nerves caught up with us. We both crashed out in the back seat.

◆ ◆ ◆

We woke up to the sound of the phone ringing on the car speakers. I opened my eyes, completely disoriented. It was dusk, and I was in an unfamiliar car on an unfamiliar road with a driver I'd barely met. The only familiar sight was Andréa, and seeing her quickly grounded me in reality.

"Agents," Jerrold said, "I have bad news."

I sat up. "Did something happen to Danielle?"

"Nothing like that," he said. "She's perfectly healthy and safe. But she made it to the contest site in time."

"What?" Andréa asked.

I checked the time on my phone. It had only been five hours.

"We sent one of our local operatives to put the contest under surveillance," he said. "Whenever Danielle arrived, we wanted to make sure she didn't just run off again after finding out she'd been disqualified. Amani, your mom arrived at the venue and inquired about Danielle only to find that she'd already checked in."

"But how is that even possible?" I asked.

"Did she sneak onto a plane under a different name?" Andréa asked.

"I take full responsibility," Jerrold said. "We were checking for trains, planes, and buses. We didn't even consider helicopters."

"Helicopters?" I asked. "How did she possibly get hold of a helicopter?" I had ridden in a helicopter on my first mission, and it was a wild and scary ride. Had she carjacked someone for a helicopter? Was helicopter-jacking even a thing? Was "helicopter-jacked" a word?

"Like I said, it's my fault," Jerrold said. "Remember that I mentioned that Sheila works for Execu-Fetch? They have a very high-level option to pick up clients in a helicopter, and apparently Danielle utilized it. Her mother is furious, because it costs thousands of dollars, even with her employee discount. But worst of all, Danielle is back on track to perform her song in front of millions, including the billionaire who runs the contest."

"Monty Hughes," I said.

"Exactly," Jerrold said. "He is the last person on earth we want to hear those song lyrics. We have to find a way to stop this. In a few hours, the team will meet up at our Northern California headquarters. We'll be putting together a new plan. You two should sleep in the car if you can, because it's going to be a long night."

We signed off with Jerrold, but from that moment on, the two of us were wide awake.

TWENTY-EIGHT

We arrived in San Jose, California, when it was dark but not quiet. With the traffic, it took us longer to go the final twenty miles of the trip than it had the previous hundred. Finally, we arrived at the Factory's makeshift headquarters, a boxy building in a suburban office park.

Jerrold met us at the car in slacks and a button-down shirt with the sleeves rolled up. It was the first time I'd seen him in anything but a suit and tie. He motioned for us to go in as he had a final word with the driver.

Inside, I was relieved to see my parents. I hugged them both and introduced them to Andréa.

The four of us sat at the table in a small conference room, and then Jerrold came in and began the briefing.

"Carmen," he said to my mom, "do you want to start us off?"

Mom nodded and stood up. "When I learned that

Danielle was in, I tried to gain access to the concert. But because Sound Cake—the K-pop supergroup—will be making an appearance, security is extremely tight. And there's no way to get a ticket. The concert is exclusively for teenage participants in these camps, so you can only get in if you're in one of the winning bands. Security has names and photos of all the band members. Noelani and Casey are on the list, and I confirmed that they eventually arrived—also beating the deadline. Amani and Andréa, unfortunately, you're *not* on the list anymore. We think there will be industry professionals on the second night, but those lists are also really tight."

Jerrold nodded, then turned to us, the teenagers on the team. "Amani and Andréa, your new mission is to go to the big concert and find a way to keep the band from revealing too much. The concert will be broadcast to millions via social media, so it's critical that you succeed."

Sure, I thought. No problem. How on earth did Jerrold think we'd be able to do that?

Jerrold turned to my dad. "Forrest, can you take it from here?"

Dad nodded and pulled up his laptop. "Our team has been doing recon on the security," he said, and shared his screen with the monitor on the wall. It showed a big map of a mansion. The floor plan of the building itself indicated a rectangular area with a courtyard in the center. There was a private road that circled around the building and the grounds.

“There has to be some way in and out of the venue,” Dad said. “Our local operative, Shawn, is there now. We have a feed from him. We want you to see what he sees. Stand by . . .” He took out his cell and dialed. “Shawn, are you there? . . . Great. I’m pulling up your feed now.”

The view changed to a video of a wooded area, where we could barely make out Shawn’s face in the dim evening light. He was a light-skinned Black man in his thirties I had never seen before.

“Okay, Forrest,” he said, “I’m changing to the glasses cam.”

Suddenly, the feed changed again. Through his camera glasses, we could see the pavement of a brightly lit parking lot. Then he was walking down a path to a wrought-iron gate.

“This is the back entrance,” Dad said.

As Shawn advanced, we saw a security guard inside a kiosk.

“Good evening,” Shawn said.

“Sorry, sir,” the guard said. “No one in or out.”

“This is where Sound Cake is appearing, right?” Shawn asked.

“Tomorrow night, but it’s not open to the public,” the guard said.

“My daughter is a megafan,” he said. “She and one of her little friends are planning to sneak in. They may already be in there.”

The guard shook his head. "It's not a public concert, sir. They can watch the live stream from home, but no one can get in, other than the contest winners. What's your daughter's name?"

Shawn gave a fake name, and the guard verified that it wasn't on the list.

"Hmm," Shawn said, sounding worried. "Couldn't my daughter and her friend have snuck in, pretending to be in one of those contest-winning bands?"

"No, sir," the guard said. "They have photos and a roster, and everyone has to show ID."

"You don't know my daughter," Shawn said. "She doesn't quit. There have to be some people going in and out. Press? Caterers? Something."

"No, sir," the guard said. "Everyone is on a roster and must show ID."

"But what if one of the waitresses stepped out for some reason?" Shawn asked. "I'm telling you, my daughter would try to bribe her with a couple hundred dollars."

"Wouldn't work," the guard said. "Once anyone has entered—including the staff—we don't allow them to go in or out unless they have a special stamp."

"A stamp can be forged," Shawn said.

"Not this one," the security guard said. "Give me your hand."

Shawn put his hand out, and the guard stamped it.

It was a blue unicorn—just a line drawing of dark blue ink on Shawn's light brown hand.

"So now I could just go to another gate and get in?"

"Nope," the guard said. "That's the stamp from yesterday. It's after midnight. This is no longer good."

"This is nothing," Shawn said. "My daughter could charm someone into showing her the stamp, take a photo, and draw it on her own hand."

"No, she couldn't," the guard said. "Because when she would try to come in, we would look at it under this light."

The guard flipped on a blue light just outside the kiosk window and guided Shawn's hand under it. The moment the blue light hit the stamp, we could see silvery wings on the unicorn, turning it into a Pegasus.

"That's a special UV master security-grade paint. It costs hundreds of dollars, and it's not available in any stores. No teenager is going to be able to get access to that on short notice at an evening concert."

"Okay," Shawn said with a grimace. "You've convinced me. I'm not sure *where* my daughter and her friend snuck out to, but it's obviously not going to be here."

"That is correct, sir," the guard said. "Have a safe night."

Shawn headed back to the parking lot. He pulled out his cell phone and switched off the camera glasses.

The video feed on the screen went blank, but we heard Shawn's voice.

"Did you get all that?" he asked us.

Unfortunately, we all got it.

TWENTY-NINE

A half hour later, Jerrold had confirmed that the Factory had access to the special ink. He was having a bottle sent to our HQ via courier.

"Ideally," Jerrold said, "we would get both Amani and Andréa into the concert."

"That unicorn was pretty detailed," my dad said. "I don't know that any of us could replicate it. The only way to forge the stamp would be to have someone who could draw something really intricate on the spot."

"The Factory has forgers who could do it," Jerrold said. "But none of them are teenagers. They would stick out too much."

"Maybe if they were in the parking lot?" Mom said.

"I guess so," Dad said. "But it's far from optimal. Look at the map again. The main entrance is here, on the other side of the property. They would have to go all the way around to the parking lot. It would take ages."

"Could Andréa skateboard?" Jerrold asked.

"No," Dad said. "It's not all paved. Part of it is a wooded path."

"So you just need someone who can draw on the spot?" Andréa said. "A teenager, who's really good and quick?"

"Yes," Jerrold said. "But none of our teen agents have that particular skill."

Andréa and I exchanged a look. I knew what she was thinking.

"We know someone," I said.

"Another teen agent?" Jerrold asked.

"Not exactly," I said. "Someone from our previous mission."

"Ramón from Arizona," Andréa clarified. "Like I said in my debrief, he already sort of suspects something from that mission. But he hasn't told anyone."

"And how can you be sure?" Mom asked.

"As part of my cover from that assignment, I've texted with him a bunch of times," she said.

"I remember approving that," Jerrold said.

Andréa had olive skin and had been out in the sun a lot at camp, but I could see her skin turning slightly redder.

"Can I confer briefly with my colleague?" she asked.

"Your colleague?" Jerrold asked.

"Amani," Andréa said.

"Certainly," Jerrold said. "Do you need the room?"

"Not at all," Andréa said. "Can we step outside?"

"Of course," he said.

I followed Andréa out into the hallway.

"I can't do it," she said. "I'm supposed to be professional. I can't just tell them that he is kind of my boyfriend and would be incredibly happy to come see me on a moment's notice."

"I can do it for you," I said.

"Do I have to be in the room?" Andréa asked.

"Yeah," I said. "You need to have the info."

She folded her arms across her chest and began to slowly shake her head.

"Look," I said, "it's really late and we're all tired. We need to finalize this plan."

Andréa sighed. But then she brightened a bit. "Can I wait in the hallway on speakerphone?" she asked.

"No way," I said. "I won't have you out here all alone while we talk about you."

"Maybe we could both call in," she suggested.

"Call in to the room next door?" I asked.

"Amani," she said, "I can't face a room full of adults on my spy team to talk about my boyfriend. I will seriously die of embarrassment."

"Yeah," I said, nodding. "I can see that." I pulled out my phone. "Okay," I said, "here goes."

"Right this second?" she asked.

"Rip off the Band-Aid," I said. The phone was ringing.

Dad picked up. "Amani?" He sounded confused.

I kept a straight face. "We are reporting in from our location in the hallway," I said. "Can you put us on speaker?"

"From the hallway?" Dad repeated.

"Can you put us on speaker or not?" I asked.

"Uh . . . sure," he said. "You're on speaker."

"Ramón is amazing," I said. "I think he would be ideal for this mission. Andréa and he made a powerful connection on the mission in Arizona. If the Factory offered him a ticket to California, he would jump at the chance. I know he could do this."

Now Andréa was definitely blushing.

"He would have to fly out tomorrow. How do we know he would drop everything?" my dad asked.

I took a breath. "Because . . . they like each other, Dad."

Andréa buried her face in her hands.

"Ohhh," Dad said.

"And we wouldn't need to brief him on the full details of the mission," I said, talking fast now. "He could be an asset, and Andréa and I would handle him. We could let him know that his participation would be conditional on him not asking any questions. The mission isn't dangerous, so we don't have to worry about Ramón's safety."

I waited for a response, but the line was quiet. "So what do you say?" I asked.

"Team?" Jerrold asked through the phone.

"I don't like it," Dad said. "We don't know this kid. The fact that we could fly him to Northern California on a moment's notice and provide such high-quality supplies will let him know that we're a significant operation."

"Yeah," Mom said. "But what's our other option? Have Danielle spill everything on live TV?"

"I'm inclined to agree with Carmen," Jerrold said. "Even if we decided to escalate the operation, how would our team even get in to extract Danielle? We could have someone parachute in, but that's not going to be easy, because she certainly isn't going to leave willingly. You're right that Ramón is a risk, Forrest, but I think it's our best move."

"I can see that," Dad said. "Can I at least do a background check on him before we make the offer?"

"Good call," Jerrold said. "Done and done. Hallway team," he said with a chuckle, "come on back in so we can make our final plan."

THIRTY

The next afternoon, Andréa and I stood watching passengers arrive at San Jose Mineta International Airport. Mom was outside, posing as a rideshare driver, and the two of us were keeping our eyes open for a Latino teen of medium height with curly hair and tawny brown skin.

He finally arrived, and I smiled when I saw him. But next to me, it was like Andréa had been hit with a bolt of lightning. She squeezed my hand and bounced on her heels. She was smitten! And the feeling was mutual. When Ramón saw her, he lit up as well.

During the ninety seconds it took for him to say goodbye to the flight attendant and come out from the secure area, I got a chance to contemplate this love thing . . . or romance thing . . . or chemistry thing . . . or whatever you call it. That whole situation with Casey had been such a fiasco. I confess, I did feel a little envious when Ramón came out through security and dropped his bag on the floor and hugged Andréa tight. It wasn't that I liked *him*—it was that I wanted someone special in my own life. But I was still happy for my friend, and even happier that we had someone on the team who could help us out of a serious jam with this hand stamp.

After the two of them hugged, it got a little awkward for a moment.

"Welcome to California," I said. "Have you ever been here before?"

"Nope," he said, slinging his bag back over his shoulder. The three of us started walking toward the exit. "But there's a first time for everything. First visit to the West Coast." He lowered his voice to a whisper. "First time on some kind of super-secret teenage crime-fighting team."

"That is so untrue," Andréa whispered back.

"What?" Ramón asked, still keeping his voice low. "You're not secret crime-fighters?"

Andréa shook her head. "We're not all teenagers."

"Exactly," I said. We walked up to the gray hatchback at the curb, which waited in the rideshare area. I rode shotgun, and Andréa and Ramón climbed into the back. Once we were safely inside the car, I said, "Ramón, this is my mom, Carmen."

My mom waved from the driver's seat. "Nice to meet you, Ramón," she said. "Welcome to the team."

"So," he asked as we pulled away from the curb, "are

we going to the secret headquarters for my briefing?"

"We were just gonna talk about it in the car and go to Burger Barn," my mom said. "If you're hungry."

"Definitely," Ramón said. "They didn't serve anything on the plane, and I didn't get a chance to eat a decent breakfast after waking up to your message that my 'artistic services were needed in California.' What does that even mean?"

"Our team has some urgent business," I said, "and needs access to a high-security location. We need a teenager who can easily imitate a dual-ink hand stamp. Andréa and I thought you could do it."

"A hand stamp? I think so," he said. "You all are providing the ink, right?"

"Of course," I said. "How quickly do you think you can draw it?"

"Depends on the intricacy of the design and how many hands I need to draw it on," he said.

"Just the two of us," I said, pointing to Andréa and myself.

"Let me show you an example of the design," Andréa said, pulling out her phone.

She showed Ramón the design of the unicorn/Pegasus.

"Easy peasy," he said.

"But that was last night's stamp," I said. "Tonight's will be different."

"Oh, I get it," Ramón said. "You need me to do it

on-site because you can't do it ahead of time."

"Exactly," I said. "It's a private concert with several youth bands and an appearance by Sound Cake."

"Sound Cake?" he said. "We're sneaking in to see Sound Cake?"

"Not all of us," I said. "Andréa and I will be going into the venue to handle some business. Meanwhile, you'll be driven back to the hotel."

"Too bad," he said. "But no big deal. Kyle is the one who's Sound Cake's biggest fan." He turned to my mom. "Kyle is my housemate."

Of course, my mom already knew that from reading the file from the case where we'd all met previously.

"I only know their music because Kyle plays it all the time," Ramón said. "He'll die when he learns that you all are seeing Sound Cake."

"Except he won't die," Andréa said mock-sternly, "because he won't know. Because this is all totally confidential."

"Right," Ramón said. "Okay. Copy that. Ixnay on the Ound-say Ake-cay."

We laughed.

"So here's the plan," I said. "We dress like teenagers going to a concert. Then we stand around with the various other teens who will be waiting to catch a glimpse of the band. When someone goes in with the return stamp, Ramón will follow them and take a video."

"Why me?" he asked.

"Because you won't be going in," I said. "When you get to the gate, they'll turn you away because you *don't* have the stamp. It would look suspicious if you didn't and then you came back fifteen minutes later and you did."

"Good point," he said.

"We'll find a quiet spot where you'll paint the stamps on Andréa and me. Your artwork will get us into the venue, and we'll handle our business. Then we'll catch up with you at the hotel later tonight."

"Sounds good," he said.

"Any questions?" I asked.

"How far is Burger Barn?" he asked. "I can't forge hand stamps on an empty stomach."

We fed Ramón two different meals that day before he found himself standing in line outside a mansion in the woods with the Factory's camera glasses on. Andréa and I stood at the barricades with the other screaming fans. According to the girl next to me in the goth Hello Kitty top and silver feather boa, Sound Cake hadn't arrived yet.

Andréa and I had been dropped there by an off-road vehicle that had roared up a wooded path on an incline. But most of these teens had hiked three miles up the hill to wait to catch a glimpse of Sound Cake through a tour bus window. That is some serious fandom.

It was just starting to get dark. Andréa and I kept looking down at our phones. Unlike the other fans, who were checking Sound Cake's social media accounts, we watched the glasses-cam video feed as the guy in front of Ramón put his hand under the light. What began as a brown panther turned into a snow tiger, with the iridescent paint making the lighter stripes.

Sure enough, when Ramón attempted to get in, the guy turned him away. Five minutes later, the three of us were off to the side in a shaded area, where no one could see us. Ramón was painting our hands with brown panthers that turned into iridescent snow tigers that looked just like the one in the video.

After we had our stamps, Andréa and Ramón hugged goodbye. Then Ramón began the long trek around to the back entrance of the mansion, where the van was waiting.

At the entrance, there were two lines. One said ENTRY and the other REENTRY. The first line had a clipboard with a list of authorized people who could enter, and they were checking IDs and stamping hands.

Andréa and I walked up to the reentry line and waited our turn. Looking at the stamps in front of us, I felt confident that we'd be fine. But you never know.

Two people ahead of us. One person. Now it was Andréa's turn. She put her hand under the blue light, and the panther suddenly was mostly white with black stripes.

"You're clear for reentry," the security guard said.

And just like that, Andréa and I were in.

THIRTY-ONE

We walked up the U-shaped driveway, in between manicured hedges. They probably looked pristine and opulent during the day, but they just looked looming and creepy at dusk. The massive building had wide double front doors, and we walked right in.

We were halfway there. But we knew that inside, there would be an additional checkpoint to get to the highly secured backstage area, and that was a problem. The other problem was that we couldn't let Danielle, Noelani, or Casey see either of us.

We had planned ahead, though. We both had on black jeans and wildly painted shirts, designed with different Sound Cake album covers and images. We looked like megafans. But once we got inside, we asked for the bathroom.

The cheerful young woman at the artist check-in

desk pointed us down a hallway. The bathroom was as fancy as the rest of the mansion, done in peachy marble with rose-gold fixtures.

In the stalls, we each took off our shirt and turned it inside out. Although one side was colorful, the other side was all white. We tucked the shirts into our pants and—voilà!—we had gone from megafans to waitresses.

It wouldn't get us all the way backstage, but it was a start.

In the movies, someone is always sneaking into a room on a room service cart with a tablecloth over it. Unfortunately, in real life, even the tiniest girl can't hide under a handheld tray of appetizers.

Our team did, however, have the layout of the house, so we knew that the in-home theater was on the second floor, which meant that the sound booth and backstage areas should be up there, as well. The problem in a mansion is finding the staircase, especially when the building is an open rectangle and the first-floor hallway seems to go on forever.

We each picked up a mostly empty tray of appetizers and strode purposefully down the hallway.

After walking the wrong way twice, we finally found an elevator with a staircase tucked behind it.

Fortunately for us, the upstairs security checkpoint was set up to keep people out of the theater and backstage—the area where Sound Cake would be—but it didn't seem to encompass the sound booth. We set down our trays and huddled in the hallway over the blueprint on my phone. After taking a few minutes to get oriented, we figured out which way to go. Circling around the other direction, we made our way to the sound booth. As we hoped, there was no security there, just a lock on the door. But Andréa was good with lockpicks.

I stood guard at the corner. Our signal was that I should cough if anyone came along. Andréa had just started to work on the door when a young woman came down the hallway toward us. I was about to cough when she opened another door and disappeared.

I heaved a sigh of relief. And then I heard a hiss behind me.

"I'm in!" Andréa whispered loudly. I turned back around and hurried in through the open sound booth door behind her.

Our plan was simple: we would plant an overriding device on the soundboard. We could activate it remotely to interfere with the sound during the performance. It would add just a little bit of feedback that would drown out the sound of key lyrics, like "CIA/FBI/KGB," "Shot down on that Charleston road," "army of Black people." By the time we were done, Danielle's performance would just be a daughter singing a series of complaints about her mother. No one on the live stream would be thinking of spies. And Monty Hughes would never have a chance to hear the real lyrics.

Andréa was using the camera glasses to share live footage of the soundboard with our team. They would be researching which channel to use for the interference bug. My job was to find the set list to know when Danielle's band went on.

The place was kind of messy, but mostly with empty energy drink cans and a few pizza boxes. There wasn't much lying around in terms of paper.

Finally, I found a clipboard hanging on the wall. As I skimmed through it, I got both good and bad news. The good news was that Flex Five went on second to last. That was great, because it would give us more time to get everything ready. But the bad news was really bad: the set list had Danielle's band doing a different song than the one we knew. I showed it to Andréa.

"How are we gonna know when to play the feedback when we don't even know the song?" I asked. The new title was "Hit and Run."

She bit her lip. "Maybe it's the same song," she suggested. "Maybe they just changed the title."

"Maybe," I said. "But we can't count on that."

I called it in to Dad.

"This is not good," he said.

"But maybe we can still fix it," I suggested, thinking out loud.

"What do you have in mind?" Dad asked.

"We need to go backstage and find Danielle's notebook," I said.

"What if the song isn't in there?" Andréa asked.

"If not, then maybe it's one of Casey's songs," I said. "Which would be fine."

"But how are either of you going to sneak backstage?" Dad asked. "The band will recognize you."

"True," Andréa said. "But there's another teenager on the team whose face they don't know."

"No way," Dad said. "You want me to send in a totally untrained teen operative?"

"Dad, what choice do we have?" I asked. "The concert is in two hours. I think it's our only play."

The line was silent for a moment.

"Dad," I asked, "are you there?"

"You can vouch for this kid?" Dad asked quietly. "He seems okay, but this means we'll have to really read him in to the mission."

"Yes," I said, "I totally trust him. We can do this if we work together."

"And I'll talk to Jerrold about maybe recruiting Ramón," Andréa said. "I know he's gonna be great."

Dad sighed. I heard him walking across gravel and opening the van door. "Young man," he said, "Amani and Andréa are assuring me that I can trust you with an additional task . . ."

But while Dad was talking with Ramón, Andréa and I realized that we had yet another problem. One of us was supposed to wear the cam glasses to work with Dad to bug the soundboard. But if Ramón was going in to get Danielle's notebook, then *he* needed the cam glasses, which meant that we would somehow need to figure out how to do the sound sabotage live.

"How on earth are we going to figure that out?" I asked Andréa. "And how are we even going to get Ramón in through security to the backstage?"

"One thing at a time," Andréa said. She coached me to take a deep breath. She breathed with me.

It helped my body calm down a bit, but I was still really worried.

Half an hour later, Andréa was hiding in the tech booth, and I was going to the front of the mansion to meet Ramón. (We had wanted to do it the other way, but I didn't fit under the soundboard.)

I was still in my waitress outfit, so on my way to the front door, I grabbed a tray of sparkling apple cider.

I walked up to the young woman at the security checkpoint. She was checking in all the VIP guests. "My manager said to send this up to you," I said.

"I can't drink on my shift," she said.

"Of course not, girl," I said. "It's just juice."

"Awww," she said. "So thoughtful."

I set it on the table to her left. When she went to take a sip, I swiped one of the VIP badges from the other end of the table.

"Have a good night," I said.

She sipped her juice as I pocketed the badge and offered juice to some guests as they came through the doors.

A few minutes later, Ramón walked into the venue wearing a baseball cap. Needless to say, he had the hand stamp and had gotten in easily.

"Sparkling cider?" I asked.

"I'm allergic to apples," he said. "Do you have any plain sparkling water?"

"Sure," I said. "Come with me."

I had texted the apple allergy idea to the team.

Ramón looked nervous as he followed me down the hall. "I don't understand why I need a baseball cap," he said. "No one knows me here."

I chuckled. "The cap is for me."

I set down the tray on a table in the hallway, then I put on the cap.

"So I'm supposed to steal someone's notebook?" he asked.

"Backstage," I said. "I'll walk you over that way."

We moved down the long hallway and took the stairs to the second floor. I held my breath as I flashed my VIP badge at the checkpoint, but they waved us through.

Inside the upstairs security area, there were different musicians and roadies carrying instruments through the hallway.

Ahead of us, the door to the women's restroom opened, and out walked Noelani. She was dressed in her performance gear and was wearing lipstick. I pulled the cap lower over my face and turned in the other direction.

Even worse, Casey came out of the men's room and headed toward us. He had on a fringed leather jacket and looked ready for the stage, as well.

I hunched down next to Ramón, the cap still low over my face. Hopefully, Casey would be too preoccupied with the contest to notice me. I clung to Ramón's arm, slouching so that nothing would give me away, not even my height.

To Ramón's credit, he seemed to take it in stride.

My heart was banging in my ribs as we passed Casey. All I saw were his black combat boots, and I felt a few fringes on the jacket brush against my arm. But he didn't stop or say anything.

I didn't dare look up or turn around. I had to just take it on faith that I hadn't been spotted.

"Follow those two artists," I said to Ramón. "I can't let them see me. We'll coach you via the glasses cam." I slipped him the glasses and the VIP pass.

He nodded and turned around to follow Casey and Noelani. I kept walking.

"Ramón is headed into the green room," I reported in to the team when I reached a quiet spot. "Pull up the cam."

Taking out my phone, I accessed the feed and looked to see what he saw.

Casey and Noelani flashed their ARTIST passes to a guard standing beside a door that said GREEN ROOM. The guard nodded and the band members walked in.

"Do I follow?" Ramón muttered into the comms.

"Definitely," Andréa said.

Ramón flashed his VIP pass, and the guard let him through, as well.

Ramón walked into a sort of big rec room full of nervous teen musicians. It had lots of couches and a few game tables: pool, table hockey, and even Ping-Pong. On the far end was a buffet table of cold cuts and sodas.

Danielle was sitting on a couch picking at a turkey sandwich. She also had on her performance outfit and a full face of makeup.

Casey was following Noelani over to the pool table.

"Danielle," Casey said over his shoulder, "stop stressing. Either eat your food or come play with us."

"I just can't," Danielle said. Beside her, on the couch, was her plaid backpack.

"Do you see the bag?" Andréa asked into the comms. "It's—" She stopped abruptly.

I waited for her to continue, but she didn't say anything.

"Um, Ramón, the backpack is plaid," I said. "Andréa, report if you can. Andréa?"

I listened, but she didn't say anything.

"Andréa," I said, "please report."

I was listening with all my concentration, but I heard only slight static.

That could mean just one thing.

"Team," I said, "the sound guy probably came into the tech booth. Andréa, I assume you can hear me but you can't talk. Sit tight. I'll keep you posted."

On the cam feed, I saw Noelani walk over to Danielle.

"Girl," Noelani said, "when you let yourself get so nervous, your voice seizes up. Come on. Just one game."

Danielle was resistant, but she let herself be pulled up from her seat.

When she and Noelani walked over to the pool table, the view from the glasses cam indicated movement. I assumed Ramón had walked over to the other end of the couch, away from where Danielle's pack was lying half-unzipped.

Ramón's gaze stayed on the pool game. Noelani was pretty good. She was playing against both Casey and Danielle. They got two shots to her every one shot, and still they were losing. Partly because Casey was so terrible. He sunk two striped balls when their team was solids. But things really took a turn when Danielle accidentally sunk the eight ball.

"Nooooo!" Casey wailed, smacking his forehead.

"Yaaasss!" Noelani crowed.

In that moment, when the crew was totally distracted, Ramón leaned over. He stayed facing the game, but I heard the sound of him unzipping the backpack the rest of the way. Then he took off his glasses and pretended to be cleaning them, but he pointed them at the backpack.

"Oh my God, Ramón," I said. "You're a natural."

"Copy that," Dad said.

"It's the notebook with the clouds on the cover," I said.

Ramón put his glasses back on and seemed to lean back against the couch.

We watched through the cam as Noelani racked up the balls for another game.

Then Ramón quickly scooped up the notebook and headed out of the room. The cam dipped for a moment, as he nodded to the guard on the way out.

I held my breath as he strode down the hallway.

"Where do I go now?" he asked.

"The men's room," I said.

He walked in, and there was a guy at the urinal. Ugh. Nobody wants to see that.

But Ramón kept walking, cool as you please, and slipped into the stall.

"You're doing great, Ramón," I said, and meant it.

He opened the notebook, and as he flipped through it, I suddenly felt bad. This was Danielle's songbook. Her private journal. Not only was someone flipping through it, but three other people were watching on a video feed.

He turned the pages slowly, so we could see the titles at the top. Finally, he found a page that said "Hit and Run."

"Stop!" I said. "That's it."

"Do I take pictures?" he asked.

"Yes," I said. "Just move slowly through the next five pages. The glasses will capture it."

We watched the feed as he turned the pages. Really, he could have just done three pages, but I wanted extra. Then he flipped through the rest of the notebook, which was blank.

"Great work," I said. "Can you put it back?"

"Roger that," Ramón said.

A few minutes later, I had downloaded the images and was reading through the lyrics of the song when I heard Ramón's voice, loud and strong.

"Did someone drop a notebook?" he asked.

Through the glasses-cam feed, I could see his hand in front of him, holding it up.

"Oh my God!" Danielle said, rushing over. "Yes, that's mine."

"Cool," Ramón said. He handed it to her, totally calmly. "It was on the floor by the couch."

"Thank you so much," she said.

"No problem," he said. "Good luck tonight."

"Nice," Dad said over the comms.

"Ramón," I said, "can you meet me outside the bathrooms? I need that VIP card."

"Will do," he said.

Outside the women's room, we brush-passed the exchange.

As I turned down the hallway, I kept scrolling through the lyrics on my phone, hurrying back toward the sound booth. I had been half hoping that the topic would be unrelated, but if anything, this one was even more specific than the previous one.

Suddenly, there was a thunder of applause.

"Andréa," I said, "I have the lyrics, but the show's starting. We won't be able to plant the device to do it remotely. We'll have to do it live."

I waited, hoping against hope she'd be able to answer. But it was still just static.

"Dad," I said into the silence, "we've got to figure out a plan to get in there and run the interference sounds."

"I don't know, Amani," Dad said. "Give me a minute to think."

Again, there was just the hissing of the line.

"Do you hear that static on the line?" Dad asked. "Could someone else be on our frequency?"

I heard the sound he was talking about. But it didn't seem to be static. It seemed more . . . rhythmic. Sort of like someone was scratching out a beat. Three scratch beats and a pause. Three beats and a pause. "Andréa, is that you?"

The beats got faster.

"Of course!" I said. "You couldn't make any noise until the concert started, but now you can!"

Scratch. Scratch.

"Okay," I said. "One scratch for yes, two for no."

Scratch.

"Is there more than one person with you in the sound booth?"

Scratch. Scratch.

"Good," I said. "Just one."

"What would get a sound tech out of a booth during a concert?" Ramón asked.

"I have no idea," I said.

"I'm looking this guy up," Dad said. "Sound tech guy . . . Did you get a look at him, Andréa?"

Scratch.

"Tall white guy?" Dad asked. "Balding. Skinny?"

Scratch.

"Okay," Dad said. "That's our guy. Brad. Not married. No kids . . . So we can't really call with an emergency from home . . . Maybe he has pets . . . Can't tell . . . Wait! He's apparently got a fancy car—a Reisinger."

"I saw one of those on the way in," Ramón said.

"Lucky break," Dad said. "I'll bet it's one of only ten vehicles allowed to park here by the front gate."

"Great!" I said. "I could go to the tech booth and tell him his car alarm is going off."

"Excellent!" Dad said.

I rushed up to the booth and knocked on the door.

A tall, skinny white guy opened the door with a scowl on his face.

"Brad?" I asked.

"Why are you interrupting me?" he demanded.

"Your car alarm is going off," I said.

I waited for him to rush out the door, but he didn't. Instead, he picked up his phone.

He scrolled a bit, then put it down. "Not mine," he said. "The app says it's fine."

"Sorry," I said. "My mistake."

I turned to leave, but suddenly, Ramón rushed in. "Brad," he asked breathlessly, "isn't that your Reisinger? Some crazy Sound Cake fans broke in to take selfies."

"What?" Brad said, and hustled us out of the booth. He closed and locked the door behind him before he ran down the stairs.

We could still hear his retreating footsteps when the sound booth door opened and Andréa ushered us in.

"That'll only hold him for so long," I said.

"I have an idea," Andréa said. "Ramón, you flew on a plane today, right?"

"Yeah," he said.

"Did you bring gum for the takeoff and landing?" she asked.

"Actually, yeah," he said, pulling it out of his pocket.

"Chew some," she said. "Then go out and stick it in the keyhole in the door. It'll hold him off for a while."

“I like it,” I said.

Ramón walked out, and we locked the door behind him.

Andréa and I turned our attention to the soundboard.

“How will we extract you?” Dad asked through the comms.

I looked around. “There’s a window,” I said. “We’ll have to climb out.”

“Copy that,” Dad said. “Good luck.”

“Okay,” I said, scanning the lyrics. “I think we just need to do the feedback for ‘Black army of spies,’ ‘Dayvon O’Malley’ and ‘Charleston alley.’ ”

“What about that last verse and ‘Black army’?” Andréa asked.

“You’re right,” I said. “We need to do all four.”

The band just before Flex Five was a Christian rap duo from Michigan. They looked like wannabe-gangster young Black men but were “on fire” for God and wanted to “murda” the devil. I couldn’t pay full attention to them, but it was a bit distracting at the edge of my consciousness.

The next thing I knew, the audience was applauding and Flex Five were getting set up.

Noelani strode onto the stage, grinning. Casey had his signature arrogant strut. And Danielle seemed confident, as well. But when she went to adjust the vocal mic, I saw that her hands were shaking.

Meanwhile, they had a new guitarist—a shaggy-haired white guy who sort of loped onto the stage in a black T-shirt and faded jeans.

And Danielle seemed so different. In rehearsals, when playing keyboards, she had been so bossy. But as the lead singer, she clutched the microphone stand with a bit of a death grip, and Noelani was the one to count off the song.

"One, two, three!"

I didn't recognize the melody, but the band was tight. I suspected that maybe it was one of their old hits being remixed or repurposed. My heart was in my throat as Danielle began to sing.

I knew how the first verse was supposed to go:

My mother joined a Black army of spies, she
turned our life into a drive-by
She dealt in secrecy but in our family she kept
secrets from me

But instead, the opening line sounded like:

"My mother joined a ***LOUD FEEDBACK***
she turned our life into a drive-by."

Yes! One down, three to go.

THIRTY-TWO

Halfway through the song, the sound tech banged on the door.

"Is someone in there?" he demanded.

Andréa and I looked at each other.

"Whoever did this is in so much trouble," he said. "Not only will your band get kicked out of the contest, but we will press charges."

In all our anxiety to block out the lyrics, I hadn't even thought about that. Our fingerprints were on everything.

"The song!" Andréa hissed.

I looked back down at the lyrics and realized we had nearly missed the second set of cues.

It was supposed to be:

A ghost with the fake name Dayvon O'Malley
Was there when you were shot in that
Charleston alley

"Now!" I hissed back, and she hit the feedback sound.

"A ghost with the fake name ***LOUD FEEDBACK***
Was there when you were ***LOUD FEEDBACK****"*

"Dammit!" the sound tech roared, banging on the door some more.

"I'll do the last one myself," I hissed to Andréa. "You need to wipe the room for prints everywhere you touched." I had only touched the interior of the doorknob and the desk. But my parents had kept any identifying information about me out of the system. So my prints couldn't be traced back to me, but hers might be.

Andréa pulled out a handkerchief and began wiping down all the surfaces, including the interior doorknob. She also spent some time under the soundboard.

While she took care of that, I returned to the final line. It was written as:

A Black army was supposed to set us free
But instead it took my parents from me

But it came out:

"***LOUD FEEDBACK*** *was supposed to set us free*
But instead it took my parents from me"

"That's it," I said. "That's the final cue."

"Look!" Andréa said. "I found some latex gloves while I was wiping everything down."

"Yes!" I said, and we both put them on.

"I did the best I could," Andréa said. "Hopefully, I got everything in here, and Ramón's print on the gum and the doorknob won't be readable."

We crossed the room to the window and prepared to climb out. Even though I had the mansion layout in my mind—a thick square building with a center courtyard—I was still disoriented when I looked out the window.

We had planned to climb out and make our way down into the garden. There had to be a place with a hedge or a tree or something we could shimmy down or that could break our fall.

"Okay, girls," Dad said, "time to bail out."

Unfortunately, as we went to climb out, Sound Cake arrived. They were walking across the courtyard, and there were bright lights and lots of press.

"It's too populated and bright out here," I said. "We'll definitely be seen."

"What do we do?" Andréa asked.

"I think we should stay put and wait for Sound Cake to leave the courtyard," I said.

"I don't like it, Amani," Dad said. "What if things stay busy and bright out there for a while?"

"Do you have a better plan?" I asked.

"Let me check something," Dad said. "I'm going

back to the floor plans. There's a helipad on the roof. I'll ask Jerrold if the Factory can get us a copter, just in case you get trapped up on the second story."

"Copy that," I said.

Then there was nothing to do but wait in the tech booth.

Flex Five got a strong round of applause, and they took their bows. We had a perfect view of the stage and the final band, which was a Dominican girl group out of New York. I don't know if they had been placed last intentionally, but they were fantastic.

> *"Girls like us are always underestimated*
> *Yet when we leave the stage everybody's devastated*
> *Was this the better life why our parents immigrated*
> *We'll carry the first-gen burden until we've made it . . ."*

After they finished, the applause was definitely louder than it was for Flex Five.

"The audience liked them best," I said. "But I'll bet Monty Hughes influences them to pick someone else."

Andréa shook her head. "Like that climate song from camp," she said. "It was by far the best. Total Futuration posted it on Instagram. I've been listening to it."

The sound guy banged on the door again.

"I'm not kidding," he said. "Your movements set

off the motion detector. I know you're in there."

But then his voice was drowned out by a loud drumroll, and Monty Hughes was back onstage.

"Before I announce the winner, I want to introduce seven friends of mine . . ."

He hadn't even said their names, but when he said "seven," the audience went wild. Everyone knew there were seven guys in Sound Cake.

In fact, no one could even hear him say the name of their band, because everyone was screaming, and then seven young Korean men were walking onto the stage.

The energy in the room was intense. It wasn't just the noise; it was the looks on some of the fans' faces. They were reaching out to touch the band members like their survival depended on it, like a single touch of these celebrities would change their lives forever.

"What's up, California?" one of the guys said. And the crowd screamed wildly, as if each of the screaming fans was named California, and the guy was speaking to them personally.

When the crowd had finally calmed down a bit, Monty Hughes took the mic back.

"It was a difficult decision, and our talent scouts are excited about many of the acts we saw tonight," he said. "But there can only be one winner. And the winner is . . . Carte Blanche!"

Not Flex Five! I hadn't realized I was holding my breath until he said the name of the other band.

We had done it! We had kept the Factory's business from being blasted far and wide. I didn't know what would be next, but I had done my part successfully.

Andréa and I hugged each other in relief.

"So," Monty Hughes said. "Any Sound Cake fans in the audience?"

Again, there was a predictable moment of hysteria that took literally over ninety seconds to die down.

"Anyone want to hear their new song?"

More screaming.

"All right," he said, and hit a remote control. A light blinked on the console, and the syrupy strains of their latest love song came out over the loudspeakers.

I had been glancing out the window from time to time. This time when I looked out, the courtyard was much quieter.

"I think we can go now," I said.

"Wait!" Andréa said. "I have an idea."

"We've gotta go," I insisted.

"I know," she said. "It'll just take a second. Trust me."

Wearing the latex gloves, she tinkered around with the console. She was doing something on the internet. The next thing I knew, she was fading out Sound Cake's latest and putting on something else.

Out in the audience, there was a buzz. Was this Sound Cake's new song?

"No!" Monty Hughes said. "Turn it off."

"For so many years, we've taken it for granted
But there's still time to save the planet"

It was the climate song from camp! Andréa set the master control and joined me by the window.

"This way," she said, "nobody will be thinking or talking about the Flex Five lyrics that they didn't hear. They'll be talking about this."

"Brilliant," I said as we slid the window open and climbed out.

"I said, turn it OFF," Monty Hughes demanded.

"The rich and greedy conduct business as usual
But their vision for the world is shortsighted and delusional"

On the roof, we stayed in a low crouch, surveying our exit routes. "You check things out that way," I whispered to Andréa. "I'll look this way."

"It's not solutions but integrity that our leaders lack
We can build a movement to get our planet back on track
We can build a movement to take our power back"

"Dammit," Monty Hughes yelled over the sound system. "I didn't sink millions into this stupid festival so some whiny teenagers could complain on my stage. This is MY stage. I decide. TURN IT OFF!"

Except he also said a few words that someone should have bleeped out. But there was no one in the sound booth to do it.

Andréa and I circled back and compared notes.

"There's a tree on the inside of the courtyard," I said. "We could easily climb down."

"Even better," Andréa said, "there's a set of hedges on the outside. Easier to get all the way out quickly."

"Sounds perfect," I said.

But just as we turned to leave, I saw a familiar figure in the courtyard. It was Danielle, sitting slumped with her face in her hands.

"I oughta go make contact," I said.

"Should I come with you?" Andréa asked.

"No," I said. "I think this might finally be the opportunity I've been waiting for."

THIRTY-THREE

I hadn't climbed up or down a tree since elementary school, and I was significantly bigger now. I scooted carefully to the edge of the roof and moved gingerly onto the branch.

It was weird to climb down a tree without having climbed up. That was how I was used to getting acquainted with any given tree—by reaching up and pulling on each branch to see if it would hold my weight before I hoisted myself up. But on the way down, gravity was working against me.

There was one branch that I thought might not hold me, but it turned out okay. Before I knew it, I was lowering myself down from the lowest branch and dropping onto the ground.

Closer up, I could see that Danielle wasn't alone. Casey and Noelani were several feet away, all of them spaced out as if they were practicing social distancing. There was no sign of the shaggy-haired guitar player.

Noelani was looking into her phone and crying.

"It's not just that we lost, Booski," she said, using her pet name for Sarita. "It's that the winning band was so damn mediocre. What made me think that girls of color could get a fair shake?"

Ten feet away, Casey was apparently going live on one of his social media accounts:

"Yeah, guys, it was messed up. We did our best, but I think it was rigged. I know this is probably not a popular opinion, but Sound Cake isn't exactly about artistic quality . . ."

Hold up, wasn't Casey the one always talking about being more commercial? How was he going to— Wait. No, no, no, no. I was still getting distracted by his drama. Danielle was the assignment.

Casey and Noelani were both facing away from me, away from Danielle and the doors to the mansion. Good. They weren't the ones I was looking for.

Danielle looked so small, sitting down with her back against the wall and her knees drawn up to her chest. I walked over and sat down next to her on the ground.

I thought about us stealing her journal, reading her lyrics. I thought about all the ways we had invaded her privacy during the course of the mission, and the fact that I was going to try to get her to open up to me under false pretenses. I reached into my ear and took out the communicator. I turned it off and slipped it into my pocket.

"Hey," I said. "You were amazing tonight. Those judges were jerks. And Monty Hughes is only going to platform the messages that glorify his own vision."

She looked up at me, her cheeks wet with tears. Then she shook her head and buried her face in her hands.

"I think it was really brave of you to sing lead," I said. "And to really tell your story."

"Imani, what are you even doing here?" she asked, her voice muffled through her tears.

"I came to see the band," I said. "Even though you didn't win, you got such a strong response from the crowd. Danielle, you're really talented."

"I don't get it," she muttered to me through her hands. "Why are you being so nice when we kicked you out?"

"I can see that you've got a lot going on from the song lyrics," I said. "I should have supported you more. You did the right thing telling your story. I got so caught up in the contest, I lost track of what was really important."

"No," Danielle said, "I was wrong. I should have paid more attention to the competition. Because I just can't go back. I can't face my mom. What she did. That tiny apartment without my dad in it. He's been dead for years, but now I know how he died." She looked up at me then.

"My parents were spies, Imani. Spies. They legit traveled to other countries and had secret meetings. I went with them. My dad was shot in the line of duty. She lied about it."

"I got that impression from your song lyrics," I said quietly. "Are you sure?"

"Yes," Danielle said. "But it wasn't the FBI or the CIA." She shook her head. "It had some big acronym, but they referred to it as the Factory. Apparently, it was Black people or BIPOC or something. Like, what even is that? Some rogue brown-people spy organization got my father killed? I can't. I can't go back. I can't face her. I can't deal. I just can't."

She said something else, but I couldn't understand it because she was really sobbing now.

I scooted closer to her. "I'm gonna put my arm around you," I said. "Tell me if you don't want that."

She didn't say any words that I could understand, so I just moved right next to her and put my arm around her. She collapsed into my chest. She sobbed and sobbed and clung to my shirt.

I wrapped my arms around her. "It's gonna be okay," I said. "It's not okay now. You're right. That sounds sooo messed up. But it won't always be this bad."

She was saying something over and over again that I couldn't quite understand. Eventually I realized that she was asking: "What am I gonna do?"

I took a deep breath. Then I began with the speech

I had been practicing in my head for the five or ten minutes she had been crying.

"You had a plan to get out," I said. "Your plan was to win this contest. And you got really far. You got to the finals. And it's been a break from your mom, but it's not a permanent solution."

"What else can I do?" Danielle wailed.

"There have got to be other options," I said. "There's always more than one possibility. I'll help you come up with some other ideas."

"I can't believe I just unloaded all this on you," she said. "I can't believe—" She wiped her face with the palm of her hand.

"It's okay," I said.

"I— All this stuff I said." She was looking around now. "I wasn't supposed to tell anyone all that. I mean, I know I said some of it in the song, but the name of the organization and all the details—"

"It's okay," I said. "I can keep a secret."

"Thank you," Danielle said. "But I shouldn't have put that on you."

"Danielle," I said, "it's too much for one person. You shouldn't have to carry so much by yourself."

When I said that, she teared up again.

"Yeah," she said. "It's too much. It's way, way too much."

"For real," I said. "And I guess since we're talking about other solutions . . . If you can't face your mom—if it's too hard—have you ever considered therapy? Like someone other than your mom to help you process the grief?"

"My mom was trying to push that on me," Danielle said. "But it's just a way for her not to have to deal with her own stuff."

"You could both go to therapy," I suggested. "And maybe family therapy where you could work on your relationship. Together."

"What's the use?" she asked. "She won't listen to anything I say. She just keeps it moving. Keeps working."

"That's what family therapy is good for," I said. "The therapist will make her listen. And you can confront her about all of those things."

"But none of that will bring him back," she said, breaking down again.

I let her cry for a while. "You're right," I said. "None of it will bring him back. So you might want to have some individual therapy, too. To process the loss of your dad, the hurricane, everything."

"But what about confidentiality?" Danielle asked. "My mom is all about secrecy."

"Therapy is confidential," I said. "There are laws. The therapist can't share what you say except in very specific instances. You can ask about it from the beginning."

"But how are we supposed to afford family therapy,

plus therapy for me?" Danielle asked. "And if I get a therapist, I'm definitely gonna insist that my mom get one, too. We don't have money like that."

"I know someone who sees women of color for free," I said. "She does it online. We could call her right now."

"Really?" Danielle asked.

"Yeah," I said. I pulled out my phone. "Let me show you her page."

I pulled up the Factory's therapist, Dr. Pauline, and showed Danielle her video.

"Girl," Dr. Pauline said to the camera, "life can get so hectic, and emotions can be so hard to sort out. Are you anxious? Depressed? Grieving? Overwhelmed? Struggling with addictions? Dealing with difficult or unhealthy relationships? Struggles in work or school? Unpacking family trauma? Come on now, sis. You can't do this alone. Nobody can. I help women of color work through rough patches and even lifelong struggles. Give me a call. If I'm not the right person to help, I'll make sure to work with you until you get the help you deserve. Whatever your issues, whatever your financial means, I'm committed to making sure women of color get the support we deserve to thrive, have joy and connection and lives we love. Give me a call."

By the end of the video, Danielle's eyes were still shining with tears, but also maybe with a little bit of hope.

"Should we call her?" I asked.

She nodded and handed me her phone. I dialed the number and passed it back to her.

"Hey, it's Dr. Pauline," I could hear the recorded voice coming through the phone. "If this is an emergency, dial nine-one-one or go to your nearest emergency room. Otherwise, please leave a message, and I'll get right back to you."

After the voicemail beeped, Danielle got suddenly shy.

"Um, hello?" she said. "My name is Danielle and I'm—" She looked at me, and I nodded encouragement.

"I would like to maybe talk to you? I mean, I definitely would. I would like to get some help. I need help. Please. Yes. Please help me."

And then she started crying again. She sagged into my shoulder.

I took out my phone and looked up Danielle's number.

"Hi, um, this is Danielle's friend," I said into Dr. Pauline's voicemail, and gave Danielle's number.

Danielle just cried into my shoulder for another half hour.

Eventually, someone from the contest came out, an impatient young woman in an evening dress carrying a clipboard.

"Yeah, I'm sorry, but the bus is leaving to take all the contestants back to the hotel," she said.

Danielle stood up and wiped her eyes.

"By the way," the girl said to Danielle, "you were one of my favorites."

"Thank you," Danielle said.

"Your group and the Dominican girls," she said, and walked away.

"Noelani," Danielle called, "we gotta go!"

Noelani walked over. "Have you seen this?" she asked, showing us her phone. Apparently, Monty Hughes's meltdown was going viral, and DJ RayBreak had made a meme remix.

He crosscut between Monty Hughes and a toddler throwing a tantrum.

this stupid festival—MY stage!
this stupid festival—MY stage!

Every time he said "MY stage!" the toddler stomped his foot on the beat.

TURN IT OFF! TURN IT OFF!
Turn-turn-turn-turn-TURN IT OFF!

Then the toddler morphed into that cartoon character whose head was always on fire.

"That's hilarious," I said as we walked back into the mansion.

When the video ended, Noelani seemed to notice

me for the first time. "Hold up," she said. "What are you doing here?" She threw her arms around me.

After we hugged, I told her, "I came to see you guys. And you were great!"

"Aww, thanks, fam," Noelani said. Then she elbowed Danielle. "See, I told you she was good people."

"Yeah," Danielle said. "I guess so, given that she's wearing a half a cup of my tears on her shirt. By the way, where's Casey?"

Noelani rolled her eyes. "He was devastated until this cute girl came over and said how amaaazing he was. Then he was just all Mr. Humblebrag." She pointed down the hall. "See?"

I followed her gaze, and then I couldn't help rolling my eyes. Casey had his arm around the girl and was talking her ear off. The girl was tall, Black or maybe Latina, and full-figured. I recognized her as a backup singer from one of the other groups.

"Wow," I said. "I guess Casey has a type."

Danielle and Noelani both laughed.

"I could have told you that," Danielle said.

I rolled my eyes again. And unlike certain other tall Black girls, the new girl seemed to be enjoying the monologue. She was giggling and hitting him playfully on the shoulder. Ugh. *Good luck with that, boo,* I thought.

"Who're you here with?" Noelani asked. "Wanna sneak into the hotel with us for a sleepover?"

“I’m here with Andréa,” I said.

“I don’t think they’ll let you on the bus,” Noelani said. “But call us. We can meet up and sneak you both in.”

We opened the front door to see a large tour bus waiting out front.

“Let me get your number,” Danielle said. “I sort of . . . deleted it.”

“I’ve still got yours,” I said as we walked down the steps. “Remember? I gave it to Dr. Pauline.”

“Imani convinced me to do therapy,” Danielle said breezily.

“Um . . . score!” Noelani said. “We’ve been telling her—”

“Enough heavy talk,” Danielle said. “Let’s just hang out and have fun tonight.”

“That sounds great,” I said. And it actually did. “I’ll catch up with Andréa and we’ll text you.”

The girl with the clipboard ushered the two of them onto the bus. Danielle climbed up the first two steps, then turned around sharply. She rushed back down the stairs and hugged me really tight.

“Thank you,” she said.

“Of course,” I said as she reboarded.

I waved as the bus exited the parking lot. Then I pulled out my communicator and turned it on.

“Sorry to be MIA,” I said. “All is well. Ready for extraction.”

As I waited, there were still a few cars around, including the sound guy's Reisinger. It was red and looked like a futuristic race car. Security was relaxed now that the guys from Sound Cake—and their throngs of fans—were gone.

A couple of minutes later, a familiar white van pulled into the round driveway. When it stopped, I climbed on board.

"We got worried when you went quiet," Dad said. "How did it go?"

"Good," I said. "Better than good. We called Dr. Pauline."

"Actually made the phone call?" Dad asked.

"Yup," I said, grinning.

"Wow!" Andréa said. "That's just—wow."

"I have more news," I said. "But it's part good, part bad."

"Uh-oh," Dad said.

"Not bad for the Factory," I clarified. "Andréa and I got invited to a sleepover at the hotel. So it's good for the mission, but not so good for the two of you." I tilted my head to indicate Andréa and Ramón.

Andréa nodded. "You have to get to your plane," she said to Ramón. "I'd hoped we could hang for a while at the airport."

"And I was hoping maybe you would tell me a little more of what I've been involved in for the past twelve hours," Ramón said.

"Here's what I can tell you, young man," Dad said. "You've done a stellar job. If you're interested, I think all of us will be recommending you for work with us again in the future."

The van was quiet as we drove back to the San Jose airport. Andréa and Ramón held hands the whole way and leaned against each other.

The traffic seemed chill, but for Andréa and Ramón, that was probably bad news. We made it in record time.

When we arrived, they stepped outside and walked hand in hand to the terminal door. He leaned down and kissed her, and I looked away to give them some privacy.

"Did you mean what you said about Ramón?" I asked Dad.

"Definitely," he said. "I think Andréa should be pretty happy about that."

A few minutes later, Andréa climbed back into the van.

"Debrief on the way to the hotel?" I asked.

"Is there anything urgent?" Dad asked.

"No," I said. "Danielle called Dr. Pauline and had a good cry."

"Then it can wait till tomorrow," Dad said. "The rest of the ride, you all just need to congratulate yourselves on a job well done."

"This slumber party had better be fun," Andréa said.

"This might have been my only chance to see Ramón again for months."

"Of course, it'll be fun," I said. "We'll be there together."

"That's true," she said, putting her head on my shoulder. "It'll be just like old times when we were in a band together."

"Old times?" I said. "That was two days ago."

"Yep," Andréa said. "Time moves really quickly for our generation."

It was a lyric by Thug Woofer, from a collaboration he did with Deza, and Dad tried to rap it.

"Time moves quickly for our generation
Older folks need a recalibration"

"No way, Dad," I said. "What older folks need is to stop trying to rap."

"What do you mean?" he asked. "Hip-hop is over fifty years old. This is my music."

"You mean used to be your music," I said. "We've taken it over now."

I started rapping Deza's part from the last verse of the song:

"We are the ones whose minute lasts an hour
We are the ones who're coming for the power"

Andréa chimed in with me and we rapped together:

"We are the ones with the scope and the range
We are the ones to demand and win change!"

I still felt a little bad to have befriended Danielle under false pretenses. But part of it had been real. We had been in a band together. I actually liked Danielle and Noelani, and under different circumstances, we definitely could have been friends. Andréa was the only other teen in my life who knew me as both a teen and a spy, and maybe someday, if things went well with Dr. Pauline, I could be honest with Danielle, too.

Now that the mission was over, I could start by being honest about not drinking. No judgment—*do you, Danielle*—but I would let her know I wasn't into it, if she even wanted to.

I wasn't undercover anymore, so I didn't have to pretend. I was looking forward to just enjoying myself around these girls without the weight of the Factory's future on my shoulders. I had worked hard nonstop—since Georgia.

Tonight would be just for fun and celebration. I couldn't wait to hang with this crew and my bestie and just be a teenage girl.